Kiss & Blog

Kiss & Blog

ALYSON NOËL

🦁 St. Martin's Griffin 〰 New York

KISS & BLOG. Copyright © 2007 by Alyson Noël. All rights reserved. Printed in the United States of America. For information, address St. Martin's Press, 175 Fifth Avenue, New York, N.Y. 10010.

www.stmartins.com

Design by Sarah Maya Gubkin

The Library of Congress has cataloged the first St. Martin's Griffin edition as follows:

Noël, Alyson.
    Kiss & blog / Alyson Noël.—1st ed.
        p. cm.
    ISBN 978-0-312-35509-8
    1. Interpersonal relations—Fiction. 2. Popularity—Fiction. 3. Best friends—Fiction. 4. Friendship—Fiction. 5. High schools—Fiction. 6. Schools—Fiction. I. Title.
    PZ7.N67185 Kis 2007
    [Fic]

                                                                    2007006748

ISBN 978-1-250-00272-3 (trade paperback)

Second St. Martin's Griffin Edition: October 2012

10 9 8 7 6 5 4 3 2 1

For the Larkin girls—Lamia, Nalani, Kiri, Tyra, and Imara—five shining stars who inspire me in every way!

Acknowledgments

Even though the actual writing of my books is pretty solitary, there's a whole army of people who inspire me, help me, guide me, put up with me, and who patiently wait for me when the return phone calls and e-mails get sorely delayed. Those people include my agent, Kate Schafer, who's smart and funny and full of good advice; my editor, Stefanie Lindskog, who tolerates my comma fondness and is a total dream to work with; my sister, Dorice, and her husband, Bill, who not only host the best BBQ's, but who also raised those five awesome girls I dedicated this book to; my mother, whose purse is forever weighed down by signed copies of my books since "You just never know when you'll need them"; my husband, Sandy, who's so amazingly awesome that sometimes I just have to pinch myself; and all the warm, funny, wonderful people who make up my tribe of family and friends—I'm so lucky to have you!

A lesson from the monkey: The higher it climbs, the more you see of its behind.

—Saint Bonaventure

One

"Can I *please* go now?" I'm staring at my mom, willing her to stop talking and acknowledge me. But she just pushes her long wavy hair off her face, glances at me briefly, then turns back to her customer, continuing their discussion on the benefits of a totally gluten-free diet.

I roll my eyes and tap my foot against the bamboo floor. I'm sick of gluten haters. Totally over soy lovers. And don't even get me started on yoga, people who meditate, or anything certified organic. Untying my hemp apron with the words NEW DAY ORGANICS embroidered in bold green letters along the front, I wad it into a ball, and glance nervously at the clock. I'm down to just fifteen minutes until I need to be at Sloane's.

"Mom?" I whine, a little louder this time.

And when she finally looks at me, she has this big smile planted firmly across her face. But I know it's for the customer, not me. I mean, I can see her eyes. And believe me, they tell a whole different story. She gazes at her watch, and then back at me, and then her makeup-free brown eyes travel all the way over to the ball of nubby beige cloth clutched tightly in my hand. And just as her head begins a kind of slow-mo, downward descent, indicating she's just about to perform the much-anticipated "okay" nod, the little bell on the front door rings, and the spell is broken.

"Go see what they need, and then you can go," she says, smiling as she gets back to her customer and the great gluten debate.

I roll my eyes, shake my head, and don't even try to contain the sigh that escapes my lips as I unfold my apron, slip it back over my head, and get behind the counter, where I'm confronted with the three most glamorous, most important members of Ocean High School's sophomore class.

"Oh, hey," I say, smiling nervously and glancing in their general direction, since I'm so not worthy of looking *directly* at them. But they don't say anything. And I mean, why would they? It's not like they ever notice me at school. "Can I get you something?" I ask, watching as they squint through their identical, shiny black Dior sunglasses at the smoothie menu hanging on the wall behind me.

"I'll have the Purple Berry Haze with a shot of soy protein," says Jaci, whose shiny blond hair, big blue eyes, golden tan, petite frame, perfect face, and Marc Jacobs intensive wardrobe serve as valuable collateral, ensuring her VIP admission to every cool party and every hot guy.

"Exact same," say Holly and Claire. Which makes me wonder if they read the menu, or just waited for Jaci to order, so then they'd know what they want.

I push up the sleeves of my black New Day Organics T-shirt, and start tossing generous chunks of raspberries, blueberries, and strawberries into the blender, trying to ignore the fact that all three of them are now totally staring at me.

"Why do you look so familiar?" asks Jaci, learning on the counter and narrowing her eyes as she looks me over.

I scoop some nonfat, organic, vanilla-flavored yogurt out of the big plastic tub and add it to the mix. Then I mumble something about having been in the same history class last year.

But she just continues to squint, as though she doesn't quite believe it. Then suddenly she shakes her head and goes, "Omigod! You're that girl that sat in the way back!"

Okay, just so we're clear, I think we can all agree that there are two types of kids who make it a point to sit in the way back.

1. The total stoner-losers who never do their homework and almost always vanish into alternative-school oblivion before the semester is even over.

2. The sober-but-shy losers like me who live for extra-credit assignments and whose only friend in the whole school (okay, *world*), doesn't share any of the same classes, so they're forced to sit alone.

I gaze at her for a moment, amazed at how she actually recognized me, and then I glance briefly at Holly and Claire. "Um, yeah," I say. "That was me."

"But something's different," Jaci says, leaning in even closer now, so that she can get a better look. "Have you lost like, a ton of weight?"

I dump some protein powder on top, reach for the lid, and shrug. All the while trying not to cringe under her close scrutiny. Okay, so maybe I used to be a little heavier, maybe I used to wear a size nine (sometimes seven), and now it's more like a five (sometimes three). But it's only because I grew an inch and a half and lost a few pounds of baby fat in the process. I mean, to hear her talk, you'd think I'd just pulled a Nicole Richie or something.

"Seriously. You guys remember, right?" she says, turning to

consult with her clones, who just continue to stand there, giving me a blank look. "Well, anyway, you look good." She smiles. "Ten more and you'll look even better!"

I just stand there, frozen. I mean, *excuse me? Was that not the world's most insulting compliment?* "Oh, well, it's not like I'm really making an effort," I finally say, securing the lid and glancing at her briefly.

"Well, you probably don't even have to. You know, working here and all." She smiles, her eyes traveling over me, judging every extra inch.

But I just shrug and flip the switch, watching as the berries swirl into the yogurt, changing color and texture, and thinking how even though I may like to watch it from an artistic angle, it's not like I'd actually ever touch the stuff.

I prefer an all junk-food diet. See, with no boyfriend (yet), and a best friend (Sloane), who's also a geeky goody-good like me, prepackaged food is about the only form of rebellion I have—the only way to really freak out my mom. And believe me, it works. She totally bugs when she sees me eating candy bars and Pop-Tarts. And sometimes it seems like her sole purpose in life is to lecture me on how I'm supposedly "poisoning my body with man-made toxins" and "hampering my immune system with transfatty acids." Personally, I think she could use a little downtime with a Ding Dong and a Dr Pepper. I mean, isn't it enough to own an organic café? Does she really have to buy into all the hype, too?

But try telling her that. This is a woman who named both her kids after the two most depressing times of the year. That's right, my name is Winter Snow Simmons, big sister to Autumn Rain Simmons. For real. I would never lie about that. And if you haven't already guessed by now, my mom's a hippie. But not the mud-covered, acid-tripping, Woodstock concert-going kind. I mean, Woodstock was like, before she was even born. She's more like a modern hippie. You know, the kind who hates pesticides, loves yoga, and refuses to dye her hair, wear makeup, or listen to any music that wasn't originally recorded on vinyl. Oh, yeah, and she prefers riding an old, beat-up bicycle to driving a car, which believe me, is even more embarrassing than it sounds.

And my dad? Well, he's pretty much the exact opposite. But it wasn't always that way. I mean, back when Autumn and I were kids they used to drag us to Grateful Dead shows, where my mom would set up shop in the parking lot, selling her secret recipe organic muffins right out of the back of our old orange-and-white VW van. We even have some old photos of us with our faces all painted, while dancing around in oversized tie-dyed T-shirts.

But then my dad's garage band scored a Billboard Top Ten hit, and he really "let the success go to his head." Or at least that's how my mom describes it. I was pretty young, so it's not like I can really recall.

Anyway, I guess that's what eventually drove them apart. My dad started to enjoy the decade he was living in, while my mom stayed rooted in one she was too young to remember.

If that sounds like I'm kind of judging her, well, I guess I am. I mean, don't get me wrong, she's a pretty cool, easygoing mom. But sometimes I wish she'd just highlight her hair, slap on some makeup, and drive a big, "irresponsible, gas-hogging SUV" like all the other moms.

And oh, yeah, she named all of the desserts in our bakery-café after songs from the sixties and seventies. You know like "Bad Moon Rising Banana Loaf," "Piece of My Heart Tart," and "Proud Mary Pie." But not one is named after my dad's greatest hit. But then again, that wasn't even recorded until the nineties.

And as for my dad and his rock god*ness*? Well, that was all pretty short-lived. Their second album totally flopped, and now he lives in New York City, where he owns an art gallery in SoHo.

But before you get the wrong idea and think that having a

one-hit-wonder dad, and an organic bakery-café-owning mom makes me popular—think again. The only people at school who actually know my name are Sloane and my English teacher. Everyone else either ignores me or checks the seating chart.

But soon, all that will change.

When the smoothies are finally all blended and ready, I lift the glass container and carefully pour it into three (recycled) plastic cups. And as I look up I come face-to-face with Cash Davis—the single most gorgeous guy to ever walk the face of the earth.

Or at least the sidewalks of Laguna Beach.

But definitely the halls of Ocean High.

I take a deep breath and try to ignore the fact that my hands have gone all shaky, and my upper lip is now sporting major sweat beads, while my stomach is throbbing with this weird, nervous *ping*. And all of this is occurring because I've never actually been this close to him before. Not that I haven't dreamed of it, like a gazillion times. But up until now, our relationship has pretty much consisted of Sloane and me silently worshiping his golden hair, piercing blue eyes, six-foot, totally ripped, muscle-bound frame, and amazing denim-clad butt, while he remains completely oblivious of our very existence.

I glance quickly at Jaci to see if she's going to actually say something to Cash, but the way she and Holly and Claire are twirling their hair and nudging one another, it's pretty obvious that cool as they are, even they have no idea how to talk to him. Because even though those three were like the big shit in the freshman class, and are destined to reign again this year when we're sophomores, Cash Davis is in a league of his own. I mean, he's hot, he's a senior, he's a varsity football star, and he drives a Hummer. Need I say more?

I blow a strand of mousy brown hair out of my eyes and grab three plastic, domed lids to cover the smoothies, gently pushing down and trying to get a secure seal when Cash goes,

"What's the Marrakech Expresso? Is that a coffee shake?"

And I get so flustered when I hear his voice actually addressing *me*, that my already sweaty palms slip against the slick plastic lid, slamming it into the counter and sending all three smoothies soaring to the floor, one after another, like Acapulco cliff divers. And when it's finally over, the floor, the counter, and I are completely covered in a thick, viscous coating of Purple Berry Haze.

I stand there for a moment, watching as Jaci, Holly, and Claire break out in total hysterics, laughing like crazy, falling all over one another, and pointing at me.

While Cash just stands there, taking in the mess, shaking his head, and going, "Oh, man, that is *sick!*"

And me? I turn around and make a run for the back room.

Bursting through the door, I toss my apron toward the laundry hamper, watching as it slides off the top and falls to the floor.

"You missed," Autumn says, barely looking up from her drawing. "Not to mention that it's not even four yet, and no way am I covering for you." She continues to shade in the area around Joaquin Phoenix's deep, dark, mysterious eyes, which I must admit she's captured perfectly.

"Don't mess with me, Autumn," I say, grabbing a towel and dabbing furiously at my clothing, trying to rid it of Purple Berry *slime.*

"I mean it. I'm not going out there 'til the big hand is on the twelve," she says, her cute little elfin face hidden by her long, murky blond hair that acts like a screen between us.

"Whatever," I say, grabbing my bag and heading for the back door, since I can't exactly use the front. I mean, I'm like a fugitive now, running from my own humiliation.

"I'm serious! Hey, Winter? Where you going?" Autumn yells, charcoal poised in midair, large brown eyes narrowed and focused on me.

And even though it's not nice, and even though she probably doesn't deserve it, I need to lash out at someone, and she just happens to be the only one here. "None of your freaking business!" I yell, and then I slam the door behind me and hurry down the narrow alleyway, holding my breath as I pass the smelly, green Dumpsters, while hoping to avoid the creepy, skinny guy of indeterminate age who seems to be on a permanent cigarette break from his job at the corner liquor store.

But why I thought I'd be so lucky is beyond me.

"Hey," he says, taking a really deep drag and squinting at me. "Couple more weeks and those dolphin-art-buying assholes will be all cleared out. Can't wait to get my town back." He flicks the newly formed ash onto the ground, not even caring that some of it has drifted right back at him, clinging to the front of his black T-shirt and jeans.

Oh, jeez, this again. Ranting about seashell-art-loving tourists is one of his favorite pastimes. I just mumble something noncommittal and hurry past. I mean, no way am I stopping to talk with this guy. It's like he's always out here, wearing the same all-black outfit, which means he either has a closetful of black, thinks he's Johnny Cash, or (more likely) he only does his laundry like, once every six weeks. Not to mention that he totally gives me the creeps. I mean, you'd think his boss would do something about the fact that he spends more time smoking in the alley than working behind the counter. And why he thinks I'd be interested in standing right alongside him, bashing tourists, and making fun of their lame art-buying habits is beyond me.

"You can thank MTV for this mess! They're not content with destroying the music world, now they're going after *my* world! Don't fall prey to that corporate-branding crap!" he yells at my retreating back.

But I just ignore him, cross the street, and board the Laguna Beach shuttle bus. Grabbing an empty seat near the back, and praying (not for the first time) that Mr. Back Alley Smoker is not gonna be my new daddy. Because believe me, I've heard my mom say some very similar things.

Heading down Pacific Coast Highway (a.k.a. PCH), I gaze at all the little shops, restaurants, and galleries, remembering how great (not to mention, convenient) it was when Sloane lived right across the street. We spent so much of our childhood running back and forth to each other's houses, getting this toy from Sloane's or that CD from mine, that our moms used to joke about building a bridge.

But now our moms don't even talk, much less joke. Which I have to admit, still feels kind of weird. I mean, they used to be best friends, sitting on the porch on hot summer nights sipping beer and complaining about our absentee dads while Sloane and I rehearsed one of the intricately plotted plays or music videos that I wrote, produced, and directed and that she starred in. I mean, years of tap and ballet had made her a natural performer, while I, a little more cerebral and far less coordinated, felt way more comfortable behind the scenes. Though sometimes I did take the stage during the musical numbers, since I like to write songs and sing.

But after the sixth-grade "Lady Marmalade" talent show fiasco (I mean, who knew that many of the parents spoke French?), we gave up the stage. And a couple of years later our mothers gave up their friendship.

At first it was awkward, watching them go from beer-swigging gripe sessions to not even speaking, but then Sloane's mom got pregnant and married (yes, in that order), and in a matter of weeks, they moved to a swanky gated community in south Laguna, an older gay couple moved into their old space, and I became a regular on the Laguna Beach shuttle bus, making the daily commute from my neighborhood to hers.

When I get to Sloane's, I find her mom in the driveway, struggling to get a screaming, pink-clad baby Blair into her car seat.

"Sloane's in her room," she says, barely glancing at me.

I stand there cringing as I listen to Blair shriek at the top of her lungs. "Um, do you need help?" I ask, even though I have no idea how I could possibly assist, other than risking bodily harm by grabbing hold of those tiny, furiously kicking limbs and pinning the baby down. But when she doesn't answer, I just head straight into the house and upstairs to Sloane's room.

"Perfect timing," Sloane says, removing her earplugs and tossing her iPod onto her big, wood, canopy bed. "They're on their way to Mommy and Me. Did you notice the matching outfits?" She rolls her eyes.

"I didn't know Juicy made clothes for one-year-olds," I say, plopping onto her furry zebra print butterfly chair, which is one of the few things she was allowed to transfer from her old life to her new one.

"They don't. My mom had it made special just for Blair. I swear, that kid was born to be homecoming queen." She laughs.

"And speaking of." I look at her, smiling with anticipation. "Follow me."

I trail her into her bathroom, which is practically bigger than the bedroom Autumn and I are forced to share, and make myself comfortable on the edge of her oversized Jacuzzi tub.

"Okay, so this is what I got," she says, reaching into a cupboard and pulling out two bulging plastic bags that seem like they just might possibly contain the entire hair and beauty section of the Monarch Beach CVS Drugstore. "I chose Frosty Latte for you, since I figured with your medium to light brown hair color you can probably go about two shades lighter and still look natural, and then I bought Macadamia Fizz for me." She tosses me the box with a picture of a smiling woman on the front, her thick, coffee-colored hair rippling in the wind as her eyes focus directly on mine, daring me to try it.

"Are we supposed to drink this or pour it on our hair?" I

laugh, staring at the color swatches on the back and trying to imagine myself with a frosty latte head.

"And check this out, I went crazy with the lip glosses and eye pencils. I figured with your brown hair and eyes, and me being blond and blue-eyed, it should be pretty easy to divvy it all up, right?"

She pours a pile of makeup onto the rug, and we kneel down around it, sorting through it, popping off tops, and coloring on the back of our hands. And when I gaze up at her, I can't help but feel this overwhelming surge of gratitude that she's actually gone and done this for me, because it's not like she has to dabble in drugstore makeup anymore. I mean, even though she may have grown up kind of poor, now, since her mom's remarriage, she's actually pretty rich. Which is kind of like having an all-access, backstage pass to the aisles of Sephora and all the best hair salons. And even though, technically, I'm not poor, I'm not exactly wealthy, either. Not to mention how my mom would never agree to pay for stuff like this. And all the money I saved from slaving in the café all summer? Well, that's already been spent on some image-altering, life-changing school clothes.

"Sloane, thanks," I say, smiling shyly, as part of me considers telling her about the humiliating smoothie incident I'd just barely survived, while the other part, the smarter, more careful part, doesn't allow it.

I mean, we've been planning this makeover and social coup since the last day of ninth grade, so there's no way I can tell her how just one day before the first day of school and our well-planned debut, I may have already blown it.

But she just shrugs. "Please, it's way more fun this way. Besides, we're in this together, right?"

I look at her and smile. "Who goes first?" I ask, opening the box and retrieving a pair of rubber gloves, knowing that no matter what happens with our plan, whether we succeed or fail, we'll always be friends.

Two

Today is the first day in the history of my life that I woke up without a hassle. I mean, usually it's a pretty big, long drawn-out ordeal, where I hit the Snooze button the absolute maximum number of times, and even then, once it's stopped cooperating and starts shrilling, I can still manage to eke out another ten minutes just by going all the way under the blankets and placing the pillow on top of my head.

But today I rose with the sun. Partly because I was excited, and partly because I had some major prep time ahead of me.

Tiptoeing past Autumn's bed, I go into our bathroom and squint at my new frosty latte hair, which is actually more the color of tea with honey and lemon than anything resembling Sumatra blend. Then I get in the shower and perform my usual routine of hair washing, leg shaving, and body cleansing, only today, all the products are new.

"A whole new life calls for all new toiletries," Sloane had said, handing me a bag full of citrus-scented shower gels, moisturizing shampoos, and conditioners that promised to make the most of my newly minted frostiness.

And now with a towel wrapped around my head and another around my body, I'm like a fresh, blank canvas, eagerly awaiting the stroke of color that will turn me into a masterpiece. Or at least keep me from blending into the wall.

I'm sick of being invisible. Tired of being bumped in the halls without apology, of being chosen last for a team (if chosen at all), and of drooling over guys like Cash Davis who wouldn't even notice if he ran over me with his Hummer.

It's like, last year, when we became freshmen, Sloane and I were so excited about getting a fresh new start, in a brand-new school, falsely believing that we could just walk away from our former junior-high nerdiness and ease into the higher social ranks, beau monde, in crowd, A-list, popular clique, cool kids, or whatever you call them at your school. But just three days into the very first week, the roles were already cast, and Sloane and I, denied the chance to audition, stood on the sidelines among a sea of faceless extras, watching as girls like Jaci, Holly, and Claire took the parts of homecoming princess, frosh-soph cheerleaders, and collective varsity jock bait.

And after yet another year of watching everyone else have all the fun that we could only dream about, Sloane and I made a pact to do whatever it takes not to go unnoticed in our sophomore year. So we spent the entire summer holed up in her room, with an arsenal of fashion magazines, Dr. Phil books (Sloane read one, while I read another, then we gave each other the gist), that book where some guy tells you how pretty much no guys are into you (duh!), and endless TiVoing of makeover shows, including *Queer Eye,* because let's face it, good advice really does transcend all genders.

And now, leaning so close to the mirror the tip of my nose is practically pressed against it, I start applying my new makeup, beginning with a light dusting of powder to hopefully even out my skin tone (and soak up some of that pesky midday shine), followed by some goldeny-beigey-taupey-colored eye shadow, a smudgy line of brown pencil along my upper and lower lashes, two coats of mascara, a pop of peach blush, a light coat of peachy-gold lip gloss, and like a pound of concealer to cover the zit on my chin that somehow manifested itself during my sleep. And when I'm done with all that, I tackle my hair with a blow-dryer, some product, a big round brush, and my new ceramic flat iron, until it's sleek, smooth, straight, and virtually unrecognizable. Then I tiptoe back to my room, hoping I can get dressed and out of there without waking Autumn.

And just as I'm grabbing my backpack and preparing to sneak out the door, she rolls over and mumbles, "Winter?"

"Shhh! Go back to sleep," I whisper, anxious to escape, sight unseen, knowing that my extreme makeover will only spawn a ton of questions that I'm just not willing to deal with yet.

"But, what're you doing? What time is it?" She squints at the clock between our beds, and then back at me.

"I'm meeting Sloane. So just go back to sleep. You have another half hour 'til you have to be up."

"But—"

"Autumn, jeez, get a life already!" I say, in my totally annoyed older sister voice. Though I gotta admit, I feel pretty guilty just seconds after it's out.

I mean, for the most part Autumn's a pretty sweet kid. But that doesn't mean she's not annoying. It's like, I've always wanted a sister who was more like a friend and an ally, someone who would unite with me against our parents. But the reality is, I ended up with a twelve-year-old version of my mom—an art-loving, bead-stringing, vegetarian baby hippie. And most of the time it feels like a losing battle of me against them.

I walk out the door and head straight for Dietrich's, just as Sloane and I planned, figuring we could meet before school, sip some java, and strategize for the day ahead.

"Hey," I say, walking inside and finding Sloane already

waiting with two coffees and a scone for us to share. "How'd you get past your mom?" I toss my bag onto the table and take the seat across from hers.

Sloane's mom is always in her business. It's like, now that she's traded in her friendship with my mom so that she can hang with all the wealthy alpha moms who live in their new neighborhood, it seems like she's been pushing pretty hard for her daughter to do the same. And even though part of me thinks it's cool the way her mom pitches in, helping her with her hair and clothes, I mean, that's something my mom would *never* do, I also know it's part of the reason why she's not all that crazy about me. She acts like I'm holding Sloane back or something, keeping her from reaching her full social potential. And even though I have to admit how that really hurts my feelings (especially when I remember how she used to be like a second mom to me), I also feel pretty lucky that Sloane just kind of rolls her eyes, and does her best to ignore all that.

"Last night when Blair was having her usual bedtime meltdown, I told her we had an early-morning orientation." She smiles.

"Why would sophomores have an orientation?" I ask, breaking off a piece of chocolate chip scone, and popping it into my mouth.

"Beats me." She shrugs. "By the way, you look great. I like your hair like that."

"It's not too straight?" I ask, grabbing a handful and inspecting the flat-ironed ends. I mean, I'd read all about how curls and waves were supposedly back, but since that was my hair's natural state to begin with it felt kind of wrong, like it shouldn't be that easy. Like I should work a little harder, and make it do the opposite.

"No, it's good, kind of edgy." She nods.

"Edgy's not good," I say, suddenly feeling completely panicked. "Edgy's like, *alternative.* And in case you haven't noticed, there are no alternative cheerleaders, prom queens, or class presidents at Ocean High, or any other high." I shake my head and glare at my coffee, feeling like the world's biggest loser, with the world's worst odds. I mean, here I am, just entering the starting gate, and I'd already scratched.

"Relax, it looks cool," Sloane says, smiling encouragingly. "Really."

I gaze at her sitting across from me, with her big blue eyes, long blond hair, shiny pink lips, Mystic tanned skin, over-priced jeans, hundred-dollar T-shirt, and three-inch designer wedge heels, and feel a little nauseous when I realize how she totally fits in. She looks like a combination of the Olsen twins, the Simpson sisters, and that spoiled blond chick on *The Real OC*. Seriously, she looks *just like one of them*.

While I, with my stupid, edgy hair, cheap knockoff clothes, and junior-high pop star fragrance with a name so em-barrassing I'll lie if anyone asks what it is, am like some pathetic outsider on the wrong side of the velvet rope. It's like, I was aiming for cool and stylish, but somehow I ended up look-ing like the world's biggest wanna-be. I shake my head and wonder which is worse, being invisible, or being visible in the *wrong way*?

"Besides, you have to find your own unique look," Sloane says, using perfectly manicured nails to flick at a stray scone crumb.

"Unique is bad. Edgy is bad. I'm so not cut out for this," I say, filled with a massive amount of despair and self-loathing.

But Sloane just shakes her head, grabs her bag, and pushes away from the table. "Come on, time for us to get noticed," she says, as I reluctantly follow behind.

As usual, Sloane and I don't have any classes together, so I'm pretty much living for the ten-minute break between second and third period when we'll meet at my locker as planned, so we can swap stories of our social conquests, even though I really don't have anything to share. I mean, maybe I haven't had my toe stepped on or my books knocked out of my arms, but it's not like Cash Davis has asked me to go to the prom, either.

Hurrying out of my AP English class, I head for my locker, keeping an eye out for Sloane as I toss my copy of *Catcher in the Rye* inside, knowing it'll probably live there for the next three weeks since I've already read it twice before, and yes, both times by choice. And even though I realize I've just revealed what a major dork I truly am, the truth is, I love to read. And even worse than that, I like most of the books they make us read in school.

"Winter!" I look up to see Sloane coming toward me, with a huge, fake smile spread across her face.

"Sloane!" I say, all overanimated, making a big show of hugging her even though we just saw each other less than two hours ago. But let's face it, if you wanna be popular, then you have to do as they do. And I've seen Jaci and her posse go through this same lame routine like twice a day for as long as I can remember.

"Omigod," Sloane whispers, leaning in and glancing around to make sure no one's listening. "You won't even believe this. But in Algebra, Mr. Jansen goes by this alphabetical seating chart, which puts me like smack in the middle of Jaci and Claire. So when he was at the chalkboard writing all kinds of crap on it, Jaci turned to say something to Claire, but since I'm sitting right between them she looked at me and went, 'Oh, hey.' So I said, 'Yeah, hey.' And then she looked me over and went, 'Nice shoes.' So I just smiled and said, 'Thanks.' And then like, two more times after that she turned in her seat to smile at me. And then, when class was over, she looked at me and went, 'Bye'!"

I just stare at Sloane, standing before me, and she's so excited and happy, and even though I'm happy and excited for her, I suddenly feel pressured to report something too. So I smile and go, "Get this, when I passed Cole Sawyer on the way to English, he kinda bumped into me, and then he looked back and went, 'Oh, sorry bro.'"

But Sloane just stares at me with her nose all scrunched-up. "He called you 'bro'?"

"Well, yeah. But remember how last year he didn't even say sorry?" I remind her, knowing deep down inside that was hardly what you'd call progress.

But she just shrugs, and then the bell rings and she goes, "Okay, well, see you at lunch."

And as I watch her walk away, I can't help but notice how easily she blends into the crowd, and I get this awful feeling in the pit of my stomach, knowing I'm going to have to work a lot harder to match that, yet doubting I ever will.

But then I remind myself of our promise, and how we swore that if one of us got there first, she would hold the door open for the other. And knowing that Sloane would never leave me behind, I pick up the pace and head to class, determined to get there on time.

Okay, so maybe lunch wasn't as great as we'd hoped, but that doesn't mean we weren't moving forward. It's like, just last year we were brown bagging it in no-man's-land, sitting so far from the action we were practically off campus. But today, we sat right next to Table B, which I guess means we were at Table C, but hey, it was closer to Table A than we'd ever been before. I mean, let's face it, the high school cafeteria is just another form of real estate, and it all amounts to the same exact thing—location, location, location.

And when the bell finally rings at 3:35, I'm rushing out of class, speeding around the corner so I can get to my locker before meeting up with Sloane, when I crash head-on into Cash Davis.

"What the fu—?" he says, regaining his balance and glaring at me.

"Oh, jeez, I'm so sorry," I mumble, my face growing all red and hot as I lean down to pick up the pile of books I just dropped. And when I come back up to face him, books all askew and haphazard in my arms, I see that he's squinting at me. And the sight of that immediately makes my heart thump even faster, as my palms get all nervous and soggy and weak. I mean, not to state the obvious but—*Cash Davis is squinting at me!*

I just stand there, speechless, mesmerized, a complete bag of sweaty, overexcited nerves. Just taking in every flawless pore on his amazingly beautiful face, watching as his perfect brows merge together as he opens his succulent mouth to say, "Oh, man, you're that chick who spilled that purple shit all over the place yesterday." Then he shakes his shiny, beach-bleached hair, and narrows his Pacific blue eyes in disdain. "You're a fuckin' hazard, bro." Then he laughs and walks away, leaving me standing there, still red-faced, still sweaty palmed, still completely mortified, but no longer sure if I like him.

"Omigod! What did he just say to you?" Sloane says, running up and gripping my arm so hard she'll probably leave a bruise. "When I saw you two together just now I though I was gonna faint!"

I look at Sloane, staring at me with eyes all wide and bugged-out with excitement, and I know there's no way I can tell her what really just happened. How just seconds after the official end of our very first day of our fresh new start, I may have already blown it. And not just for myself, but possibly for her as well. Since after having just engaged in my second unfortunate episode with Cash in less than twenty-four hours, I think it's probably safe to assume that it's better not to be seen in my presence if you're a card-carrying member of the "I love Cash Davis" fan club.

Yet I also realize that up until now I've never actually lied to her before (well, at least not about anything important like this). But I really can't see another choice. I mean, there's no way I can risk having her know just how big of a social liability I really am. Not to mention how I can't bear for her to think that maybe her mom is right, that maybe I really am holding her back, and keeping her from realizing her full social potential.

So I just take a deep breath, avoid her eyes, and shrug like it was no big deal. "Oh, that? He just ran right into me." I laugh, hoping I sound both carefree and convincing, which would be the exact opposite of how I really do feel.

"But what did he *say*?" she asks, still gripping my arm, still gaping at me.

"Well, he said he was sorry, then he tried to help me pick up the books I dropped." I bite down on my lower lip and look away. *Man, I totally suck at this.*

"Okay, but you have to tell me *everything*!" she says, steering me toward the parking lot. "Starting from the very, very beginning, leave nothing out."

And when I look at her, I see so much admiration and excitement in her eyes that it makes me feel horrible. But that doesn't mean I confess. "Well, I was turning the corner and he just smacked right into me," I say, gazing down at the ground as we head toward home.

Three

"And while we totally wish that each and every one of you could make it, the sad fact is, there's only room for six," Ginny says, gazing out at her audience and bestowing us with her adorable, sad kitten look, which only results in me elbowing Sloane, as I roll my eyes and laugh under my breath.

But Sloane just sits there, doing her best to ignore me while smiling and nodding at everything Ginny says, like she's a true believer or something.

So I turn and gaze around the room, wondering if I'm the only one who sees through all this phony-baloney nonsense. But when I notice how they too are all caught up in the rapture of Ginny, it's clear that I am.

"Pay attention, this is important," Sloane hisses, glancing at me just long enough to show some major disapproval.

So I face back toward the front, focusing all of my attention on Heidi, Ginny, Krystal, Shelby, Tatiana, and Lori, who are not only famous for being the six hottest seniors who rule the school, but also for making up the entire varsity cheerleading squad. Then I smile wide and nod like I mean it, trying my best to imitate Sloane, and act like I too am just another member of the recently converted. Like I too am someone who truly believes that these six girls really want nothing more in this entire world than to exalt us all to their rarified status.

Only, the thing is, those plastic smiles that are currently plastered across their perfect photogenic faces really don't match the cold, judgmental gleam in their eyes. And it's almost like, if you just look and listen closely enough, you'll actually start to wonder if maybe, what they really wish is the exact opposite.

But it's not like I share any of that with Sloane. Instead, I just continue to nod and smile and laugh when I know I'm supposed to, partly because I don't want to annoy her any more than I already have, and partly because it's good practice for when we both make the junior varsity cheerleading squad.

Sloane and I are pretty excited about these upcoming tryouts, as we both agree it's the ultimate shortcut, the quickest, most direct route we could think of to Table A status.

I mean, drill team? Dog squad.

Class president? Nice on a college application, but not exactly hot.

But a girl in a short skirt with pom-poms? Show me the guy who can resist.

And since Sloane has been taking dance classes practically since she took her first step, she's like a complete natural at performing, choreography, jumping around, and stuff. And since I like to write songs and sing, I'm in charge of the lyrics. We even worked on a few potential moves over the summer, in anticipation of this exact moment. So I guess we're both feeling pretty confident about our odds of making it.

Besides, it's not often that you get a second chance like this. I mean, last year, during J.V. tryouts, we were feeling so low and down on ourselves that we didn't even go to the meeting, much less make up a cheer. But after that nasty judging scandal forced school administrators to revise the entire voting process, making it less political, and more fair (kind of like they had to do with Olympic figure skating), people who don't normally get a fair shot at these things, people like Sloane and I, will now, under the protective umbrella of the threat of legal action, actually stand a chance.

"So, tryouts are Monday at four. That gives you just five days to practice your cheers," Tatiana says, tossing her long, dark hair over her shoulder and dazzling us with her perfect, Crest Whitestrips smile. "So, everyone, just try to work hard but *have fun!*"

That last "have fun" part was said by all of them. And I watch in amazement as they all just sort of naturally lean in, heads close together, like they're posing for the world's cutest group photo.

I look over at Sloane, who is gazing at them in awe, watching as a swarm of girls rush them, like orphans to Angelina Jolie, and I go, "So, you wanna go back to your house and practice?"

But she just shakes her head, gets up, and heads straight for the receiving line. And I, unable to see any other option, just stand up and follow.

When it's finally her turn to speak, Sloane smiles and says, "Omigod!" And then tentatively reaches out to touch Ginny's hand. "I just *love* your ring! Where'd you get that?"

And since up until this exact moment I hadn't even noticed she was wearing a ring, I scoot in even closer, peeking over Sloane's shoulder and peering at Ginny's bejeweled finger. But still, all I can see is just a thick, silver band with three small purple stones across the front, and as I stand there and stare at it, I can't help but wonder what all the fuss is about.

But Ginny raises her hand up high, gazing at it with unabashed admiration, then she looks at Sloane and smiles and goes, "Thanks, Spence just gave it to me."

That would be Andy Spence. The Lincoln Navigator–driving, USC-bound, varsity-footballing best friend of Cash Davis, who for some inexplicable reason, goes by his last name.

I just stand there and watch as Sloane leans even closer to the ring, making me wonder if she's gonna get down on her knees and kiss it, like you do with the pope. And then I look at Ginny, and the way she's gazing at Sloane reminds me of how I sometimes look at Autumn (when we're not fighting). You know, that kind of adoring, protective, big sister look. And as I'm watching this unfold, I suddenly realize how even though it all seems kind of comical and phony to me, it's also pretty obvious that something very important is happening here. That this is actually a very critical moment in our social strategy. That with one, well-timed, perfectly delivered, half-hearted compliment, Sloane has managed to take one giant leap forward for both of us.

And then Ginny's eyes meet mine, giving me this expectant look, and knowing I have to say something, too, or risk looking like a lame retard mute, I lean in and go, "Oh, yeah. It's so cool! Really, totally cool." And even though I nod vigorously and smile with all my might, I can tell she's not buying it.

"Okay, well, good luck," she says, turning away dismissively, focusing her attention on the fans waiting impatiently behind us.

"So," I say, grabbing my backpack and following Sloane outside. "What do you think? My house or yours?"

But Sloane just storms ahead without answering. And just as I'm thinking she didn't hear, and I'm about to repeat the question, she turns on her heel and shakes her head. "Winter, I can't even believe you," she says. "That sounded so fake just now." She looks at me with her lips all grim and her eyes all judgmental and harsh.

But I just shrug. "Please. You wanna hear fake? How about 'and while we totally wish we could choose each and every one of you'!" I mimic, shaking my head and laughing out loud.

"Shhh!" She glances around frantically, then looks at me and rolls her eyes. "Omigod, just tell me, once and for all, do you want to move forward with this or not? Because to be honest, it's starting to seem like you don't." She folds her arms across her chest, in a perfect example of defensive body language 101.

"Of course I do! But come on, you gotta admit, a lot of this stuff is just *so fake*!" I laugh. "I mean, be honest, you didn't really like that ring, did you?" But when she looks at me, shaking her head and narrowing her eyes, I know I may have gone just a teensy bit too far.

"I'm totally serious," she says. "You so don't get it. If you want to be in with these people then you have to like what they like. And I don't mean to be a bitch, Winter, but no one is going to appreciate your little sarcastic comments. So you need to decide, right now, what it is you want to do. *Because I'm getting in, no matter what!* I've worked way too hard, and this is way too important to just give it all up because you've suddenly decided that everything is just some big, phony joke. So tell me, what's it gonna be? Are you in, or are you out?"

She's standing there, arms still folded, and I know that she's totally serious. Which, I admit, kind of makes me feel a little sick. I mean, Sloane has been my best friend forever, so not only is this ultimatum more than a little surprising, but it's also knocked me totally off-guard. And, the worst part is I'm starting to wonder if maybe she's right. I mean, maybe my sarcasm really is holding me (us) back. Maybe I am just this awful person who's always looking for the punch line, and who gets her jollies by mocking this wonderful group of optimistic, well-meaning girls who truly do love this school and every single person in it, and who are just naturally happy and high on nothing more than unmitigated school spirit and goodwill toward all.

Not to mention that Sloane is right. If I'm sick of being a nobody, if I truly want to move forward with our plan, then I need to learn to relax and just go with *their* flow.

So I look at her, feeling a little shaky and nauseous inside, but grateful that there's still enough time to save my sorry self (from myself). "I'm in," I say, in a small, tight voice, nodding so she'll know just how serious I am. "Totally, completely in."

"Good," she says, just as her mom pulls up in her silver Lexus SUV. "Now, let's go practice at my house."

"Where were you?" my mom asks, as I toss my backpack onto the kitchen table, and head for the fridge.

"Sloane's," I say, ducking my head inside, trying to locate something to eat that's not good for my heart, won't aid my digestion, and will do absolutely nothing to stop the onset of osteoporosis.

"Dinner will be ready soon, so don't fill up on junk," she warns.

I roll my eyes and close the fridge. As if filling up on junk was even an option in this place. I mean getting crazy around here means biting into a conventionally grown apple.

"So how's school going?" she asks, turning away from the stove so she can look at me.

"Day two, and nothing to report." I shrug, watching as she stirs something thick and red that I vote "most likely to end up on a heaping plate of gluten-free, soy pasta." Then I unzip my backpack and sort through my papers, until finding the one that I need. The one that requests her signed consent so I can dash her dreams, break her heart, and totally let her down by trying out for cheerleader.

But now that I'm holding it in my hand, I just stand there, staring at it, thinking that maybe I should just bypass her completely, smuggle it into my room, and attempt to forge her signature or something since I know damn well that there's no way I'll ever get her to agree to this. I mean, the only organized activities she ever approves of are either political or environmental. And let's face it, making the squad certainly won't benefit anyone other than me.

And just as I'm about to shove it back in my bag, she looks at me and goes, "What's that?" And then she squints at it from across the room, like she can actually read the small print from all the way over there.

"Um, well, I just need you to sign this. Just right on that line there. It's no big deal, so you don't even have to bother with reading it or anything," I say, knowing I'm completely blowing it by acting all nervous, and overexplaining, because, let's face it, that's pretty much always a dead giveaway.

"Well, what is it?" she asks, rubbing her hands on her jeans and reaching for her reading glasses.

I just stand there, anxiously watching her face as she reads it over, trying to gauge what her response will be. And with her lips pressed all firmly together, her eyes all narrowed, and her jaw gone all tense, I know it's not gonna be good.

"Oh, Winter, are you sure you want to do this?" she asks, gazing at me with a whole lotta concern and more than a little disappointment.

But feeling surprised by her question, and fearing it's a trap, I just nod without blinking.

She looks at me for a moment, and then lets out a sigh that's thick with resignation. "Okay," she says, voice full of defeat. "Just get me a pen."

So I reach into my backpack and hand her a pen. And as I watch her sign on the dotted line, I know that this was just way too easy, and I'm braced for the inevitable lecture, the oft-repeated "free to be you and me, evils of conformity, corporate America is trying to homogenize us but we won't let 'em" speech. But surprisingly, it never comes.

She just hands me the paper and goes, "Can you set the table for dinner? It'll be just the two of us tonight, your sister has art class."

And as I head for the drawer where we keep all the natural fiber, vegetable-dyed placemats, I peek at my mom, waiting for something more. But she's back to stirring the sauce, adding a pinch more thyme, and humming "Scarborough Fair" under her breath.

The next day, I'm hanging out at my locker during the ten-minute break, eager to show Sloane the words to our cheer, which I finally finished during a *Catcher in the Rye* discussion in AP English. And I start to feel kind of anxious when I realize that break is almost half over and yet there's still no sign of her. And after shaking my head and rolling my eyes, and basically just showboating my annoyance for the whole school to see, I suddenly remember that if I want people to like me, then I need to clean up my act, and suppress any and all emotions that don't convey extreme happiness, wholesome sexiness, and out-of-control school spirit.

So I make my posture a little straighter, smooth the wrinkles from my white Mossimo T-shirt, and tug on the waistband of my two-hundred-dollar Rock & Republic jeans that I totally splurged on even though I definitely couldn't afford to. Then I concentrate on looking super, deliriously happy, which only results in me feeling like an idiot, standing around and smiling like that for no apparent reason.

And just as I shut my locker and decide to go find Sloane, I see her approaching me. But it's not until after I call her name and wave that I realize she's not actually heading for me at all. In fact, she doesn't even seem to be looking for me. She's just walking along, taking her time, while all of her attention is focused on Ginny.

"Hey, you guys!" I say, smiling and rushing toward them, wondering if this moment requires one of those big fake hugs, or if it's better to just hang back and let one of them make the first move.

But Sloane and Ginny just keep talking, as if I'm not even there. So I search Ginny's outfit, quickly scanning it, looking for something to compliment since I saw firsthand just how well that strategy worked for Sloane. But since she's dressed in her cheerleading sweater and skirt and those white, extra-support tennis shoes (the same kind you see on nurses and the elderly), I know it won't seem authentic. And since the last time I attempted this I totally failed, I'm really feeling the pressure to get it right this time, or not do it at all. And after looking her over a second time and realizing there's nothing for me to compliment that won't come off as either totally dumb or completely creepy, I settle for just standing there, like a total retard, waiting for one of them to notice me.

So then finally Sloane gazes up at me and goes, "Oh, Ginny, this is my friend Winter."

And after barely acknowledging me, Ginny turns back to Sloane, gives her a meaningful look, and says, "So, *remember.* Okay?"

And Sloane nods, her eyes locked on Ginny as though some very serious information has just been exchanged.

I watch as Ginny turns to leave, and I know I need to contribute something quick, so I cup my hands around my mouth and go, "Bye, Ginny!" And I sound really animated when I say that, just like Sloane and I practiced all last summer.

But Ginny just totally ignores me and disappears around the corner. While Sloane shakes her head and says, "Omigod, *why'd* you just do that?" Then she glares at me, complete and total scorn plastered right across her face.

"Do what?" I ask, feeling really confused. I mean, jeez, why is she so upset? I was only trying to be polite.

But Sloane just grits her teeth, and whispers, "Yell good-bye like that."

"Um, because she was leaving and that's what people do when someone takes off." I shrug, wishing we could just move past this so that I can show her our final cheer.

But Sloane just looks at me and rolls her eyes again. "Ugh, this is so impossible!" she says, turning to walk away.

"Sloane! Wait! Where you going?" I chase after her. "Listen, I finished our cheer and I want you to see it."

But she just hurries away from me as fast as she can. "I'm going to class. I'll see you at lunch," she says, without once looking back.

By lunch, everything's normal again. We're sitting at Table C, I'm eating a healthy sandwich that my mom made especially for me, and Sloane is sipping a Diet Coke (or "liquid candy, don't kid yourself" as my mom refers to it), while she reads the cheer.

"This is really good," she says, glancing up at me and smiling.

"Really? You think?" I ask, taking a bite of my free-range turkey and organic Swiss on whole grain, while gazing at her.

"Totally. I think this is really going to work. Can I keep it?" she asks, already folding it up and shoving it deep inside her purse.

"Um, I guess," I say, feeling really weird about feeling weird to see her just taking it like that.

"Because you know how I need to have the final words so I can make up the final moves." She smiles, looking right at me.

And then just as I start to ask, "So what's the deal with Ginny?" Jaci, Holly, and Claire stroll by on their way to Table A. And all three of them glance at Sloane and say "Hey," while totally ignoring me.

I watch as they pass and then turn toward Sloane, shaking my head as I look at her. "Wow, looks like you're moving right along," I say, my blatant admiration ringing loud and clear.

But she just looks at me and shrugs. "I'm trying."

Four

After school, I'm standing in the kitchen, sipping from a bottle of water, and watching as Autumn outlines a fresh new sketch of Jonathan Rhys Meyers's amazingly sculpted face for her Tuesday afterschool portrait drawing class, when the house line rings.

"Omigod, I can't believe you turned off your cell!" Sloane says, skipping right past hello and heading straight for the recriminations.

I just roll my eyes and lean against the counter, wondering if this is why she's calling, so that she can lecture me on popular cell phone charging protocol.

"Whatever, anyway," she continues. "I'm on my way to South Coast Plaza and I need to know how soon you can get there?"

I gaze at the kitchen clock on the far wall, and sigh. Technically, I'm only about twenty minutes away. But that's only if my mom is willing to dust off the car for such an extravagant excursion as going to the mall (and have I mentioned that it's a *hybrid?*). And I'm feeling kind of annoyed by this because, well, partly because I'm feeling kind of annoyed by just about everything these days, but also because Sloane already knows all of this. She is fully and completely clued in to all of the little minute details, all of the ins and outs, and hows and whys of my pathetic day-to-day life. So I can hardly believe that I have to explain it to her, yet again. I mean, between best friends, some things should just be *known*.

"I'm not really up for the mall," I say finally, choosing the cop-out over the explanation.

But she's not going for it. "Not an option," she snaps. "Beg, borrow, steal, I don't care what you have to do, or how you do it, just get there!"

Jeez, she sounds just like that agent guy on Entourage, I think, shaking my head and wondering why some stupid trip to the mall is suddenly fraught with such monumental importance.

"Jaci, Holly, and Claire are going to be there and they want us to meet them in Sephora in thirty, no, make that now twenty-eight minutes," she says.

"Um, *us,* Sloane? Really?" I shake my head and roll my eyes, and don't even try to hide my skepticism.

"Okay, fine. So they actually invited *me*. Well, now I'm inviting *you*. Just like we agreed. So I ask you, once again, how soon can you be there?"

"Fine, give me thirty, thirty-five minutes tops," I tell her, hanging up, and wondering how on earth I'm going to pull this off.

It sucks being fifteen. For so many reasons I can't even begin to list them all here. Though I will state, right now and for the record, that at the very top of my list of Things That Suck is the word *driver's license,* and the fact that I don't yet have one. Nor do I have one of those moms who just lives for the moment when school lets out so she can pick up her kids and proceed to cart them all over town, from one place to another, for as long as they damn well please.

And since my mom actually grew up in a time long before SUVs and car pools were even invented, way back in the days when kids who lived within walking distance of school were expected to do just that, and then get on their bikes and pedal like mad if they wanted to have any kind of a social life after three o'clock, she, unfortunately, is under the impression that what was good enough for her then is surely good enough for Autumn and me now. And even though I suspect that my dad is probably modern and hip enough to completely disagree with her antique, time-warp, child-rearing philosophies, it's not like he lives here, so he's really not much help.

So now, I find myself in the very regrettable position of having my social life for the next three years resting on a single trip to the mall, where my only hope of getting there on time (if at all) depends on a woman whose values belong in the Museum of Antiquated Beliefs.

I pick up the phone, fully prepared to do battle, when my mom, once again, takes me by surprise when she sighs. "Oh, Winter, do you really need to do this?"

So I just sigh right back and say, "Yes, Mom, I really do."

And thirty-eight minutes later I'm breezing into Sephora with the ten bucks my mom slipped me riding securely in my front pocket, even though I'm fully aware of how it probably won't buy me much more than a tin of sample-sized lip balm.

"Hey," I say, approaching Jaci, Holly, Claire, and Sloane who are all huddled together in the Too Faced aisle.

But the only one who says "Hi" back is Sloane. And to be honest even that sounds pretty halfhearted, like she just couldn't afford to risk any possible deduction points by getting all happy over the arrival of someone like me.

"So which do you like better?" Jaci asks, balling her hands into tight little fists, and shoving them toward me so that I can inspect the lip gloss stripes she's painted on top.

And as everyone huddles even closer, waiting to see which one I'll pick, I suddenly realize that this is like a pretty big deal, and actually far more important than it seems. So I lean toward her outstretched fists, noticing how the one with the red-blue undertones is far better suited to her skin (which is actually pale white and *not* Mystic brown like she wants you to think). So I point at that one and go, "Um, I think that one, right there. Yup, definitely that one," I say, nodding for emphasis, and feeling pretty confident that I totally aced this little test and made the right choice. I mean, let's face it, this isn't just some crazy, random, eeny-meeny-miney-mo decision, this was actually based on years of art classes and color theory immersion courses that my mom enrolled me in until I was old enough to revolt.

But Jaci just stares at it, her nose all scrunched up, and I know that even though, technically, I'm right, obviously, that's not at all how she sees it. "Well, I hate to break it to ya, but I'm getting this," she says, pointing at the pink one with the heavy yellow undertones that'll only succeed in making her look jaundiced and lipless. But it's not like I can actually tell her that, so I just sort of nod and shrug, fully aware of how it's a lot better if I don't say anything now.

And then, of course, right on cue, Holly and Claire go, "Oh, yeah, definitely the pinker one, so much better than the other."

And then they both look at me like it's a challenge, as though they're actually daring me to stand by my original choice. But since it's not my problem if Jaci's lips fade into the rest of her face, I just shrug.

So then they all turn to Sloane who's looking at me with narrowed, disappointed eyes, and an expression that says, "Don't blame me. I tried to help, but you're the moron who fucked it all up." Then she shakes her head, looks at the others, points at the yellow-pink stripe, and goes, "That one, totally."

And then, just as I'm wondering if I should expect to be escorted out by security or something, I watch in amazement as Jaci grabs two tubes of that partisan vote lip gloss and drops them right inside the opened zipper of her Gucci tote bag.

Then she looks at all of us and goes, "I am so over this place. Let's go hit Ron Herman."

The walk from Sephora to Ron Herman is actually not that far. But for me, straggling behind, and wondering if there's any real legal precedent to the phrase "guilt by association," it feels infinite.

I mean, *hello, Jaci just stole two tubes of lip gloss!*

But as we head toward the store with no sign of screaming sirens or flashing red lights, I start to relax. And then it dawns on me that Jaci just stole some lip gloss and *nobody even flinched*. Not Holly, not Claire, and even more surprising, not even Sloane, who, by the way, is now a full three steps ahead of me, and dead set on pretending that I don't even exist.

And it's like, not to sound like a pious little teacher's pet, but I just don't get it. I mean, why the Winona? Because it's not like Jaci can't afford the thirty-five dollars it might've set her back. From what I've heard her dad is like some big-time developer (or, as my mom so delicately puts it, "land raper"), while her mom has devoted her entire life to the pursuit of Pilates, pedicures, personal pampering, and parading Jaci and her friends pretty much anywhere and everywhere they want to go after school and on the weekends. So, obviously, this is not an ability-to-pay issue.

When we get to Ron Herman, I'm still lagging behind as all four of them head straight for the Juicy Couture section. And even though I guess some of that stuff is kind of cute (well, for other people, but not really for me), I gotta admit that I'm pretty much amazed at how they never seem to tire of it. I mean, just how many pastel warm-ups can a person really own before their entire closet begins to look like a big fat Easter basket?

And even though I now know that my only real shot at overcoming the whole lip gloss fiasco will require me to stand right alongside them and coo over tiny, pink terry-cloth dresses, too, I gotta admit, at this exact moment, I'm just not feeling all that up for it.

So once again, I just stand there, watching silently and trying to keep my face neutral, as they press little cotton skirts and tops against their skinny bodies, while complaining about how fat they are.

And even though I'm aware that my job as the passive observer is to deny and rebut every single self-directed insult, every single insincere self-criticism, doing my part to try to rescue them from their fake self-esteem issues, I still just continue to stand there, not saying a word. Because the fact is you could shove all four of them together and still not fill a pair of size-eight pants. I mean, I aced ninth-grade algebra, which means I'm fully aware that size zero times four still equals zero. And believe me, it's not like they don't know that, too.

"Do you not like this stuff?" Jaci asks, holding a yellow terry-cloth mini-dress with matching lace trim to her torso, and looking at me in a way that says, "If you answer wrong, you are so going down."

"Um, yeah, some of it's okay," I say, shrugging yet feeling pretty good about my answer, amazed at how I actually found a way to preserve my own, differing opinion, while still reserving judgment on her personal style choices.

"So what kind of clothes do *you* like? Because I'd be very curious to see them," she says, dropping the dress back on the rack and narrowing her eyes at me.

I gaze at her for a moment, and then I look around, noticing how they're all staring at me. Well, everyone but Sloane, who's now so totally over me that her eyes are practically glued to the ground, refusing to go anywhere near my direction.

But again, I just shrug. "I don't know, I haven't really looked around or anything," I finally say.

"Well, let's have a look then, shall we?" Jaci fake-smiles, weaving her skinny, spray-tan arm through mine, and leading me to the other side of the store where the nonpastel, less girly pieces hang. "What about these?" She holds up a pair of cool, black, sleek, stovepipe pants. "These look like something you might like."

"Um, yeah, they're pretty cool," I say, feeling surprised that I actually do mean it, and reaching out to touch the sort of stiff-looking fabric.

But just as my fingers are about to make contact, she squints at the price tag and quickly yanks them far out of my reach, her face dropping into a dramatic pout. "Oh, three hundred dollars. Too bad," she says, tossing them back on the rack. "Or, how about this?" She pulls out a plain white, short-sleeved T-shirt, again going straight for the price tag. "Hmmm." She looks at me, her lips all pressed together. "Eighty-five dollars is probably a lot more than you spend on your Mossimo's, huh? But still, just feel that cotton, such better quality, don't you think?"

She pushes it toward me, practically forcing me to touch it, but this little game is getting so weird and mean, I've decided to stop playing.

"Okay, well I think I'm gonna take off now," I say, my eyes boring into Sloane, willing her to wake up, come to her senses, and follow me, or at the very least acknowledge that I'm even here.

But when I get no response, I just turn toward the door, fully prepared to walk out, when Jaci says, "Omigod, come back here! I was *so* totally kidding!"

So I turn around and look at them, watching as they all fake-smile at me, well, all except for Sloane who is biting down on her lower lip and gazing at me in this pleading way. And I know it sounds lame, and I know that you'll probably hate me, but I don't leave. I just continue hanging with them, following them from store to store, until Jaci has stolen an entire outfit and decides to call it a day.

"Can I ride with you?" Sloane asks, as we head outside of Nordstrom to wait on the curb, where I told my mom to meet me.

I just nod. I mean, I'm definitely not feeling all that happy with her right now, but still, it's not like I'm gonna leave her stranded at the mall or anything.

"Listen," she says, looking at me for practically the first time since I got here. "I'm really sorry about all that stuff that happened back there."

"Yeah, well, you didn't look all that sorry at the time," I say, shaking my head and refusing to look at her now. I mean, I know we made a pact, and basically spent the entire summer planning and plotting and dreaming of having a moment just like that. But now that it's happened, I have to admit that it really wasn't all that great. In fact, it actually kind of sucked. And I'm starting to wonder if maybe we should just sit down and rethink all this, and try to get out while we still can.

But apparently Sloane is not on the same page, because she just looks at me and says, "You so don't get it, Winter. It's not like Jaci actually meant any of that stuff, it—it was more like a test, like an initiation or something. You know, like when you pledge a sorority and they test your loyalty level before they decide to let you in. It was totally innocent, harmless even! They were just trying to see if you could handle hanging out with them, because obviously not everyone's up for it. Believe me, they did something very similar to me right before you showed up." She nods, her eyes searching my face, trying to see if I believe her.

I look at her, wondering if that really is true, or if she's just trying to make me feel better. Or, even more likely, if she's just trying to make *them* look better.

"Just be glad they didn't make you steal something, too," she says, retrieving a brand-new Chanel black eyeliner pencil from her purse and holding it up in offering. "Want it?" She looks at me, shrugging her slim shoulders.

"Um, no thanks," I say, turning to see my mom pulling into the parking lot.

"You're not going to say anything are you?" she asks, dropping it back in her purse, suddenly sounding all scared and nervous, and a lot more like the Sloane I've known for the last eight years. The one who never ignored me, who was never mean to me, and who certainly didn't steal stuff just to impress someone.

"To who, Sloane? Who would I say something to?" I ask, feeling sad and tired and totally sick of playing these weird little head games. I mean, everything's so different now, but not in the way I thought it would be. And to be honest, it kind of makes me miss my old life, where everything was just so much easier and way less complicated. It's even making me wonder if I was actually happier than I realized. Because now, standing next to Sloane and her stupid stolen Le Crayon Yeux, I feel kind of depressed.

I just wish everything could go back to how it was before.

But that's probably only because I know it's too late.

"Okay, well, if it's any consolation, I'm pretty sure you passed. I mean, after Ron Herman, they basically left you alone, right? And I know you heard how they all said 'See you tomorrow' when they were heading toward Saks. Because believe me, if they didn't like you, they wouldn't have said anything," she says, just as my mom pulls up next to the curb in her rarely driven Prius.

"Yeah, and what does that mean? What do I get for surviving that kind of emotional hazing?" I ask, opening the passenger door, and peering at her, watching as her face breaks into a big, triumphant smile.

"What do you think? Popularity!" she says, her face all lit up as she climbs into the back.

Five

I gotta admit, the next morning as I'm making my way to Dietrich's, I'm feeling kind of nervous about seeing Sloane. I mean, that whole mall episode with the stealing and the mean little comments just felt so freaking weird that I'm seriously having second thoughts about our plan. And I'm wondering if maybe we should think about scheduling a nice, cordial, sit-down conference, where we can rehash this whole thing, admit where we may have gone wrong, and then don our parachutes and bail out early, before the whole thing goes down in a cloud of smoke.

But when I walk in the door, I see Sloane at our usual table, with two coffees and a chocolate chip scone before her, smiling and waving like everything's completely normal. And as I take the seat across from hers, I can't help but wonder if maybe I'm just overreacting, and getting all paranoid and resistant to change. I mean, maybe things aren't really as bad as I think. And maybe I'm just panicking because it's been kind of hard watching her fit in so much easier than me. Because the fact is we made a deal, I mean, we even went so far as to sign an actual popularity contract (her idea, though I'm the one who drafted it), so now I guess I'm just gonna have to pitch in a little more, and do my part to see it through.

"Hey," she says, pushing my coffee toward me, and taking a quick sip of hers. "You think Jaci will show up in her shoplifted skirt today?" She breaks off a piece of scone and smiles.

I roll my eyes and laugh. "Yeah, what's up with that?" I ask, sipping my coffee, and looking at her. "I thought her family was supposed to be like, mega-rich or something?"

"Believe me, they are," she says, shaking her head and rolling her eyes. "I don't know how she can stomach it though, 'cause when I got home, I felt so bad about that stupid eye pencil that I ended up giving it to my mom. It's like, I just felt way too guilty to actually use it, yet I also couldn't bring myself to throw it away. So I just ended up telling her it was part of some gift with purchase, and that I didn't really need it because I already had one. But I gotta admit it's kind of funny to think about her lining her eyes with a stolen pencil." She laughs.

And when I look at her, I start laughing, too. Not because it's all that funny, but because I'm thinking maybe I can start to relax again, now that everything's finally back to normal.

But by break when Sloane doesn't show up at my locker, I decide to head for hers. And when I'm halfway there I find her standing in the middle of the quad, talking and laughing with Jaci, Holly, and Claire.

"Hey," I say, smiling as I join them, doing my best to convince myself that Sloane was right, and that all that weird stuff at the mall was just part of some crazy popularity hazing ritual that I've successfully passed, and can firmly put behind me.

But the only response I get is a lazy-eyed glance followed by, "Oh, he—"

I swear, that's exactly how they say it, like it's just way too much effort to add that final *y* for someone as unimportant as me. So I just stand there, feeling my confidence plummet as they completely ignore me and continue right where they left off. And if you think Sloane, my best friend in the whole wide world, makes any effort to fill me in, or at the very least, acknowledge my presence, well, think again.

But when the bell rings, and the three of them scatter off to class, Sloane finally turns and looks at me, rolling her eyes when she whispers, "Omigod, did you *see* Jaci's outfit? I think the only thing she didn't steal was her shoes. But then again, she probably swiped those the week before!" She shakes her head and laughs. "Listen, I can't be late to English, but let's go over our cheer at lunch, k?"

And I stand there in the hall, watching as she runs to class, and then I turn around and head toward mine.

By Friday morning I'm in a total panic. During the course of the week I'd already worn every piece of clothing from my collection of knockoffs, in addition to the two items with labels that I was actually proud of, and now I find myself marching dangerously close to the much dreaded territory of *retail repeat*. Not that anyone would notice, mind you. Because even though it definitely seems like I'm blending in better than ever before, it's not like any hot guys (or *any* guys for that matter) are actually looking at me, or like Ginny, Jaci, Holly, or Claire even acknowledge my existence when Sloane's not standing right next to me.

Still, the ban against wearing the same outfit twice in one week is just one of those unwritten, yet clearly defined, completely understood, universal rules. And with Sloane showing so much promise in her bid to join the social ranks, and with our cheer coming along so well, I'm feeling pretty obligated to do whatever it takes not to become a bigger burden than I already am. I mean, I'm really doing my best to keep my mouth shut whenever I'm feeling unsure what to say (as opposed to nervously yammering on and on about nothing, like I used to do), and am even making a concerted effort to smile *all the time.* Which makes my jaw ache so bad I think it's giving me TMJ.

But now, standing before my closet with absolutely nothing to wear, I can feel myself getting worked up to the point of hysteria. And, believe me, I'm fully aware of just how ridiculous that sounds. I mean, last year I never used to worry about stuff like this, because once you're firmly shut out of everything that matters, you're pretty much free to do as you please and wear whatever you want.

But now that I'm standing on the threshold, and actually have a shot at getting in, it suddenly seems like every little nuance, every minor detail, is not only amplified, but also put right out there for everyone to see and/or *judge*. And I know that if I somehow get it wrong and mess up this early in the game, then the repercussions may very well affect my social standing for *the next three years*!

So, knowing there's just no way I can scale this peak alone, and that I'm in desperate need of a savvy Sherpa, I grab my cell phone with the full intent of calling Sloane, figuring that not only will she be able to calm me down and walk me through this, but also will help me piece together something really cute to wear. But then just as I'm about to press Talk, it suddenly dawns on me that it's probably better if I *don't* talk to her about this. Because even though she's my best friend (which pretty much means I should be able to call her whenever I want about anything I want), the truth is that things are starting to feel a little unsure and fragile lately. And I just don't think I'm in any position to ignore the voice in my head that's urging me to just snap my phone shut and drop it to the ground, nice and easy. Because if I can keep myself from calling her, then she'll never have to know just how panicky and insecure I feel. Then maybe she'll stop all the glaring, head-shaking, and acting like I'm some kind of major liability.

It's like, over the span of the last four days, I feel like I've been standing on the sidelines, watching how easy it's been for her to assimilate. And even though she swears they were just as mean to her that day at the mall, it's not like I actually witnessed it. So excuse me for wondering if maybe it's not even true. Like, maybe, buried somewhere deep down inside her Louis Vuitton purse, was a receipt for that Chanel eye pencil, and that she actually just made the entire story up for the sole purpose of making me feel better, and less like a loser.

Yet I'm also starting to notice how lately, it seems like the only time she's ever nice to me is when Jaci, Holly, and Claire aren't around. And how the second they show up, she starts totally ignoring me, judging me, and eye-rolling me again. So I guess I'm feeling pretty unwilling to do anything that might encourage that.

"I just don't get what the problem is," Autumn says, lounging on her bed in an outfit that looks more like pajamas than school clothes.

"Whatever," I say, turning to scowl at her. "It's not like I asked you anyway."

But unfortunately she's used to being scowled at by me, so it's not like it even fazes her. "Why don't you just wear those jeans you paid way too much for, you know the Rockin' Republicans? You can wear them with the white ribbed tank top, under that kind of billowy, gauzy, blue tunic top, and those three-inch cork wedge heels that you also overspent on."

I just stand there and stare at her, wondering when she became Rachel Zoe. "It's Rock & Republic, you big dork," I finally say, even though she's just given me the perfect solution. *I mean, hello? Mix 'n' match, why couldn't I see that?*

But she just smiles. "I was making a joke," she says, apparently so accustomed to my bad attitude that she's able to ignore it now. Which, I gotta admit, makes me feel so bad about being such a mean, older sister, that I make a real effort to soften my tone and ask her about school, while I change into her suggested outfit.

"School is awesome." She shrugs, continuing her sketch.

"Any cute guys?" I glance at her.

But she just laughs and makes a face. "Crosby told Marc to ask Sage to ask me if I liked him. But I said no."

I button my jeans and stare at her. *This is freaking unbelievable!* "You don't mean Crosby Davis? Cash Davis's little hottie brother?" I ask.

But she just nods.

"Why don't you like him?" I ask.

"He's not my type. Besides, I don't want to get all tied down." She laughs.

"Not your type?" I gape at her. *I mean, how can she be serious? He's like a Cash Mini-Me!*

"He doesn't even know who Jimi Hendrix is!" She shakes her head and rolls her eyes.

"Um, Autumn, I hate to break it to ya, but Mom has turned you into a freak, because most kids don't know who Jimi Hendrix is," I inform her, as I slip my feet into my shoes.

But she just shrugs. "Their loss."

I just stand there, staring at her in shock. I mean, the hottest sixth grader in Laguna Beach likes my art-fart baby sister, and she rejects him because he doesn't worship a guy who's famous for playing the national anthem—on his electric guitar—*with his teeth!*

I shake my head, grab my bag, and head out the door. I swear, life is so freaking unfair.

Since I'm the first to get to Dietrich's I just go ahead and order our usual, two coffees and a chocolate chip scone, then I carry it over to our usual table.

"Hey!" Sloane, says, rushing through the door. But this time, Claire is trailing right behind her.

"Oh, sorry, I only got two coffees, I didn't know you were coming," I say, smiling even wider for Claire's benefit and shrugging apologetically.

But she just shakes her head and waves it away. And then, gaping at my scone with her eyes practically bugged-out of their sockets, she goes, "Omigod! Don't tell me you're really gonna eat all that? That's like a trillion calories, not to mention all the fat grams and carbs!"

I gaze down at my scone, curious to see if maybe it's tripled in size since I last looked at it, but it looks pretty much the same to me. Then I glance at Claire's face, noticing how it's all scrunched up and judgmental, like she just smelled something truly awful and suspects I'm to blame. "Well, usually Sloane and I split it," I finally say, feeling totally ridiculous for having to defend my breakfast.

Claire gapes at Sloane, while Sloane rolls her eyes at me, and goes, "Please. I'm *so* off the carbs. One more bite of anything and I'll totally explode out of these jeans!"

I look at Sloane, watching as she pats her perfectly flat belly, feeling pretty awful and depressed to hear her say something as stupid as that. Because the truth is she looks amazing in her stovepipe Earnest Sewn jeans, striped T-shirt, and little ballet flats. I mean, she looks just like that picture of Sienna Miller she ripped out of *InStyle* and hung on her wall. And even though I know how a lot of girls like to whine about imaginary cellulite and pockets of fat that don't even exist, seeing Sloane acting like that is really starting to freak me out.

It's also making me wonder if maybe I only wanted to be popular in a theoretical way, but not in a real way. Like, I had fun with all the planning and shopping and decorating but now that it's time for the big move, I'm suddenly realizing that I might not actually want to live there. Because if this is what's required of us, phony smiling 'til our faces ache, avoiding food while our stomachs growl, and putting aside all of our opinions just so we can pretend to like and dislike the exact same things as everybody else—well, it's starting to feel like way too high of a price. It's starting to feel like the ultimate sellout.

But since I can't exactly say that, much less ignore the ominous look Sloane is giving me, I just break off a miniscule piece of scone, pop it in my mouth, and throw the rest away. Wondering how on earth I can possibly make it to lunch without fainting from hunger.

During the ten-minute break, Sloane shows up with Claire again. And by lunch I can hardly believe it when we're promoted to Table A. I mean, don't get me wrong, it's not like we're sitting in the center, or anywhere near the top (which is the absolute most coveted spot because then practically the whole school can see you), but we're definitely securely perched on the far outermost edge. And even though I don't really say anything, and even though nobody says anything to me, and even though I don't really like anyone here (other than Sloane), I gotta admit, it still feels pretty amazing.

After school we're all (and by all I mean, me, Sloane, Jaci, Holly, and Claire), standing in the school parking lot, talking and laughing while waiting for our rides when Cash Davis strolls by.

And the second he's out of earshot, Jaci puts her hand over her heart and goes, "Omigod, have you ever seen a more perfect specimen?"

And then Holly and Claire immediately agree and mumble something about his rock-hard ass and major tight abs. And then Sloane looks at me, who up until now, everyone has pretty much been trying to ignore, and goes, "Well, you guys, Winter actually *talked* to him."

They all stare at me, their faces bearing a skepticism that's impossible to miss.

"Seriously." She nudges me in the arm. "*Tell* them."

I glance at Sloane, wishing she wouldn't do this, even though I know she's only trying to help, and then I look at everyone else and sigh. "It was nothing," I say, trying to affect what I hope comes off as a jaded, world-weary demeanor. "So not a big deal."

"Oh, please," Sloane says, nudging me even harder this time. "Tell them how he picked up your books and stuff."

She's smiling, but her eyes are cold and hard, warning me not to say something stupid, begging me not to blow this. And just as I open my mouth so I can resurrect my lie about Cash bumping into me, Jaci, rolls her eyes, stifles a yawn, and goes, "Uh, excuse me; but the last time I saw you anywhere *near* Cash Davis was when you were freaked-out and covered in head-to-toe smoothie. So, whatever. Anyway, my ride's here. So kiss-kiss, everyone!"

I just stand there, unable to speak, as I watch Jaci, Holly, and Claire trot off toward their "ride," which is actually just Jaci's angry-looking mom, hunched behind the wheel of her highly accessorized black Range Rover, yelling into her cell phone.

"What the hell? How come you never mentioned that to me?" Sloane asks, looking pretty angry just as her own mom pulls up in her shiny, new Lexus.

I just look at her, nervously dangling my backpack from two, outstretched fingers, and wondering how I'm going to explain this. Then finally I take a deep breath and say, "Well, I started to, but—" But then I just stop and shrug, suddenly unwilling to finish my own sentence. I mean, I really don't like the way this is starting to feel. And I really don't like how, lately, I always have to defend just about everything I say and do around her.

But Sloane just exhales loudly and gives me this totally annoyed look. "Well, are you coming or not?" she asks, opening the car door, not even trying to hide her frustration.

And even though it would be nice to get a ride home, the last thing I need is to be in a confined space with her and her disapproving mom. So I just shake my head and watch as she climbs inside.

And just as I start to walk away Sloane slides down her window, hangs her head out, and goes, "Kiss-kiss!"

And I smile as I turn to face her, knowing she's trying to make up for all the tension by totally making fun of Jaci, just like we used to, before we were trying so hard to be her friend. But when my eyes meet hers, I realize she's serious. And I remain on the curb, staring after the Lexus, until I can no longer see them.

On Friday nights I usually work in the café. Which basically means that my mom is totally taking advantage of my nonexistent social life, as well as possibly flaunting some very serious child labor laws. Sometimes, I even go so far as to wonder if she's intentionally sabotaging Autumn and me, determined to raise two social retards with no life, just so she can save on overhead.

Not that Autumn's a social retard. I mean, to me she may be a major dork, but ever since learning about little Crosby Davis's crush on her, I'm starting to realize that other people don't necessarily view her in quite the same way.

I pour two Strawberry Fields smoothies into two tall glasses, reminiscing about the time when I changed all the names, updating the signs to reflect more current titles to songs that people actually listen to. Like, "Don't Phunk With My Heart Tart," "Crumbs From Your Table Crumble," and my very own personal favorite, "As Ugly As I Seem Smoothie." But needless to say, my mom was not amused. And by the very next day everything was back to normal again.

After delivering the smoothies, I head to the back, where I grab two totally overstuffed and very heavy trash bags, which I proceed to half drag and half carry all the way outside to the Dumpster, totally cringing when I see the unmistakable red glow of skinny dude's cigarette, bobbing in the dark, at the end of the alley.

"Nice out," he says, taking another drag as he approaches, nodding at me like we've been hanging out and chatting for years.

"Yup," I say, struggling to heave one of the mammoth bags into the bin and failing miserably.

"Here, let me get that." He clamps his cigarette between his lips and lifts the bag with surprising ease for someone with no visible muscle tone. "So how's school treatin' ya?" he asks, reaching for the other bag and tossing it in as well. "Learning anything?"

"Not really." I say, feeling anxious to get back inside and far away from him.

"What grade ya in, ninth?"

"Tenth," I say, feeling totally offended he thought I was a freshman.

"Yeah, well, they don't really teach you anything 'til college." He nods, blowing two perfect smoke rings, and watching as they dissolve into the night.

"You went to college?" I ask, immediately regretting the amount of surprise in my voice, but still, I didn't expect to hear that.

" 'Course I went to college," he says, shaking his head at me. "What? You think I'm some philistine lowlife, working in a liquor store?"

"Um, no, absolutely not," I say, gazing toward our back door, longing to be on the other side of it.

But he just throws down his cigarette, smashing the smoldering tip under the sole of his old, beat-up Doc Marten. "I thought you were different from all those other spoiled brats," he says, shaking his head at me. "But apparently you're just like the rest of them."

And as he shakes his head, mutters under his breath, and heads back down the alley, part of me feels kind of bad about all that. While the other part really hopes that he's right.

When I go back inside, I wash my hands, then head straight for Mr. and Mrs. Strawberry Fields smoothie. "All done?" I ask, grabbing their sticky glasses, and wiping up the mess they made with an old, damp rag.

And then, for some inexplicable reason, like some kind of ESP moment or something, I happen to look up and gaze out the window, at the exact same moment that Jaci, Holly, Claire, and *Sloane* walk by.

Oh, my God! I think, as I stand there, staring at Sloane, waiting for her to peer inside and wave at me. I mean, she knows I work every Friday night, so why else would they be here?

But just as I'm wondering if my mom will let me leave early so I can go hang out with them, I watch in shock as she just breezes right by. With absolutely no intention of stopping, waving, or giving any indication that she's in any way affiliated with New Day Organics, or me.

She just laughs at something Jaci said, tosses her hair behind her shoulder, and strolls right past, without so much as a single glance.

"Ahem, excuse me? Miss? I said we'd like two cups of the Let It Be green tea."

I glance at the woman who is now rolling her eyes and shaking her head, then I gaze out the window again. Watching Sloane laugh and joke with her cool new friends with such comfort and ease, it's like she's been hanging with them forever.

Six

On Saturday morning I call Sloane. And when she doesn't answer her cell, I call the house line.

"Yes?" the maid answers in tentative English.

"Hi, um, is Sloane there?" I ask, hoping she can understand me.

"Yes?" she says again, leaving me unsure if that's "yes, she's there," or if we're actually, like, starting this whole process all over again.

So this time I rephrase it. "Can I speak to Sloane, please?"

"No." Of this, she sounds certain.

"Okay, but does that mean that she's there but busy and therefore I can't speak to her? Or that she's not home so I can't speak to her?" I ask, realizing that even I'm a little confused by all that.

But then she goes, "Sloane very busy. She studies. With coach."

And while I'm trying to figure out what the heck that means, she hangs up.

And I just sit there, phone still in hand, thinking: *Sloane is studying with a coach? Does that mean she has a tutor? And why didn't she mention this before? I mean, usually I'm the one who helps her with her homework.*

And then like, the second I hang up, it rings. And since I know that it's Sloane, I go, "Hey, so what's with the coach? I mean, we're supposed to be practicing our cheer."

And then my dad goes, "Okay, but I lost my pom-poms so we'll have to share."

I roll my eyes, and laugh. "Very funny," I say. "I thought you were Sloane."

"Obviously. So what's this about a cheer? You trying out for the squad?"

"Yup." I plop down onto the couch, put my feet on the coffee table, and grab the remote.

"Does your mom know?"

"Affirmative." I nod, even though he can't exactly see me.

"Wow, how'd you get that past her?" He says that in a funny way, not a judgmental way. Like in a "you and I both know how she feels about the establishment and cheerleaders definitely fall into that disdainful group" kinda way.

But I just laugh. "Wouldn't you like to know," I say, channel-surfing past all kinds of shows I don't really like.

"So, when are you and Autumn coming to visit?" he asks.

I drop the remote, even though its last stop was some over-the-top religious show, and wonder how I'm gonna answer this. I mean, I like my dad, don't get me wrong, and he's actually more like a friend than a dad. You know, kind of cute and irresponsible but highly likable, kind of like Rory Gilmore's dad. And he's cool too, with the whole rock star thing and all. But ever since he moved to New York, visiting him is like a total hassle, involving a long-ass flight, and sleeping in a cramped apartment, which can get more than a little awkward when one of his revolving girlfriends decides to drop in and pay him a visit.

But I don't want to tell him all that and make him feel bad, so instead I just say, "I don't know, I guess we'll just see how it goes, you know." Then I gawk at the screen showing the flamboyant preacher in the sparkly, yellow suit, standing next to his God-fearing wife with the lavender hair, dress, and shoes.

"Okay, but I'm warning you, I already bought two tickets, with open dates on each end, and I've mailed them out so they should be there by Monday. Tuesday at the latest," he says.

I just mumble good-bye and close the phone, my eyes glued to the line of converts falling to the ground, writhing in ecstasy, as the preacher taps each of their foreheads, absolving them of sin and saving their souls, while his color-coordinated wife smiles beatifically beside him.

At four o'clock I go to Sloane's. I mean, I'd wasted my entire day calling every two hours, and either listening to her cell go straight to voice mail, or getting the run-around from the maid. And the truth is, you just can't practice a two-person cheer with only one person. Not to mention that she still has all the words, which left me in the very awkward position of winging it.

I stand at her front door, ringing the bell, and hoping, as usual, that her mom's not home, while fully prepared to do battle with the maid. So when Sloane answers, I'm actually caught off-guard.

"Hey," she says, all casual, like she was fully expecting me or something. "What's up?" She takes a sip from her bottle of water, then wipes her hand on the side of her sky-blue, terry-cloth shorts.

"Well, I thought we were gonna practice our cheer, since we're running out of time, and all," I say, feeling pretty awkward to just be standing in the doorway, and wondering why she isn't inviting me in.

She leans against the doorjamb (which pretty much prohibits any form of entry short of knocking her over), scrunches up her nose, and goes, "About that."

And as I watch her expression change, my stomach fills with dread. But I don't say anything. I just stand there and wait for what's next.

She gazes down at the ground, and then back at me, and then she finally shrugs and says, "I think it's probably better if we try out separately."

"What?" I just stare at her, my mouth hanging wide-open, knowing there's no way she can be serious. "But we've been planning this for months!" I say, hating the way my voice sounds all whiny and desperate, like I'm about to cry or something.

"Yeah, well, I just think it's better if we each do our own thing," she says, unwilling to look me in the eye.

I just stand there, gawking. I mean, I can't freaking believe this. My best friend since third grade *won't even look me in the eye*!

"Listen, practically everybody says it's better that way, Jaci, Ginny, . . ." she trails off. "Anyway, just trust me, it's all for the best." She nods.

"But that's so not true! You and I broke it down, remember? We studied all of the cheerleaders since junior high, and every single one of them tried out with a partner! The judges always fall for that phony, cutesy, buddy stuff," I say, searching her face, and wondering why she's decided to do this *now*. I mean, after all of our planning, all of our pie chart graphing.

But she just rolls her eyes and shakes her head, and when she finally looks at me, she sighs and says, "See, that's exactly my point. *You* think it's all fake and phony, but I *don't*. I really do think it's cute. And that's why I'm trying out with Jaci."

"Omigod," I say, taking a wobbly, unstable step back.

"I'm sorry, Winter. I didn't want to tell you, but I figured you'd find out anyway. I just think you should maybe reconsider, you know? I mean, maybe you're just not cut out to be a cheerleader. Did you ever think of that? It's like, you spent that entire meeting rolling your eyes, and making fun of everyone, and don't think they didn't notice." She narrows her eyes at me. "Look, this is just way too important to me, and I've worked way too hard to risk having you . . . well . . . whatever." She shrugs, and looks down at the ground.

"Dragging you down?" I gasp. "Is that what you were gonna say? *You can't risk having me drag you down?*" I stare at her, needing to hear her say it, yet fearing she will.

But she just looks at me and shrugs. And when my eyes meet hers, it's obvious that she's already moved on, that she's totally over me, and that this is just the messy, yet obligatory, breakup scene.

So I take another step back. And then I turn away. And right before she closes the door, I turn back and say, "And the coach?" I look at her, waiting.

"My mom's idea." She shrugs.

And it's not until I get home, and into my room, that I realize she still has my cheer.

Seven

That whole episode on Sloane's porch seemed so surreal that on Monday morning I actually kept to my usual routine of stopping by Dietrich's and buying two coffees and a chocolate chip scone. Can you even believe that? I guess that's what people mean when they talk about denial.

And if that wasn't bad enough, I then found myself hanging by my locker during the ten-minute break, waiting for my ex-best friend who (big surprise) never showed. And it wasn't until lunch, when I realized that I was now officially the only remaining member of Table C, while Sloane was quickly working her way closer to not just the middle, but the actual pinnacle of Table A, that the enormity of the situation finally hit me.

And I just sat there, hunched over my cooler pack, taking tiny bites of the avocado organic sprout sandwich my mom had made, while sneaking peeks at Sloane who was tossing her hair and laughing, as though she was born right there on that very table. Then I gazed around at some of the lesser tables, wondering if I could maybe find solace in some other low-rent loca-tion. Though to be honest, it didn't seem like any of them would have me either.

And when the bell finally rang at 3:35, well, I just grabbed my books and got the heck out. I mean, JV cheerleading try-outs would begin in just twenty-five minutes, and I planned to be as far away as possible when it all started.

But on my way home, I found myself stopping by the café, even though I wasn't scheduled to work. I guess I just couldn't face hanging in my room, all alone, with nothing but my sad, lonely, depressed thoughts to keep me company. I mean, I just wasn't ready to face all that. And since I'd barely spoken a word all day, I was feeling more than desperate for a little company.

Heading into the back room, I drop into a chair, and toss my backpack onto the floor at my feet. And when my mom looks up from her calculator and pile of receipts she says, "Win-ter? I thought today was tryouts?" Then she glances at her watch and back at me.

And even though I originally thought I wanted to talk, I definitely don't want to talk about *this*. So I close my eyes, shake my head, and say, "I really don't feel like discussing this right now." And when I hear my own voice, I feel kind of bad about sounding so tight and clipped and mean, but I'm also pretty hopeful she'll get the hint and move on.

But my mom, totally blind to my plight, continues. "Is everything all right?" she asks, gazing at me with concern as she swivels her chair, ready to jump up and hug me if the situ-ation should warrant.

And the fact that she doesn't get how I've suddenly changed my mind, that I'm no longer in the market for com-pany, and that my new goal is simply to be left alone, makes me so freaking annoyed that I grab my backpack and storm out the back door, cringing as it bangs hard against the frame.

And as I stomp past skinny smoker dude, I don't acknowl-edge him, and he refuses to speak to me.

By the time I make it home, Autumn is already there, and she looks at me all excited and goes, "Hey, Dad sent us each a ticket to visit him." She holds the envelope high in the air, waving it around like a starter flag.

But I just roll my eyes. "Duh," I say, sticking my head in the fridge, even though I'm not at all hungry.

"What do you mean? It was just now delivered, so how could you possibly know?"

I slam the fridge shut and look at her. "He called Saturday and told me all about it," I say.

"Oh." She shrugs, dropping the envelope onto the table. "Well, when do you think we should go?" she asks, looking to me for guidance.

But I'm not up for guiding, leading, directing, or any other kind of big sister role-modeling, so I don't even answer. I just go in our room, slam the door, and pretty much hide in there until morning.

Okay, if I thought Monday was bad, well, Tuesday? Tuesday was torture. I mean, it started out pretty much the same as any other day. I got up at my usual time, obsessed over my clothes, and stopped for coffee on my way to school. But this time I only bought one, and knowing that the usual chocolate chip scone held way too many memories, I skipped right over it and went for the snicker doodle cookie instead.

Then the second I stepped on campus, I saw them. All six of the brand-new, fairly chosen, legally vetted members of the junior varsity cheerleading squad, jumping around and acting all high on excitement, while still clad in their pajamas.

My stomach filled with dread as I watched Sloane smiling brightly and hugging everyone who mattered, all the while looking adorable in the brand-new, Victoria's Secret pj's she bought for this very occasion.

And I happen to know that for a fact, since I was standing

right next to her at the register when she pulled out her mom's black Amex, slapped it on the counter, and purchased her outfit for her date with destiny.

"Okay, so the varsity squad always, *always* kidnaps the JV squad and makes them go to school in their jammies, so we have to buy something super-cute, but not too obvious, you know?" she'd said, as I stood behind, watching as she trolled through the racks. "And it's better to avoid anything too sexy, since it's so much better to be considered adorable than slutty, right?"

I nodded in agreement, remembering the unfortunate incident just last year when one of Ocean High's newly crowned frosh-soph goddesses was sent home in shame just seconds after Principal Meyer threw his navy blazer over her sheer, mesh, skimpy cami, matching boy shorts, and sky-blue Ugg boots ensemble.

We stood there, shoulder to shoulder, poring through mounds of possible contenders, until finally settling on a pair of pink cotton pajama pants (that could easily double as sweats) with the word *Pink* written right across the butt (I guess that's for the color-impaired), and these matching, little white tank tops that said *Love Pink* down the back. Then we bought some pink bras (I know you don't normally sleep in a bra, but the tank tops were *white*), matching pink Ugg slippers (well, Sloane's were Uggs, mine were Target fakes), and then we vowed to wear our hair all pulled back in spunky, high ponytails, and to go to bed with just the lightest layer of shiny pink lip gloss (so we'd look good, but not like we were *trying* to look good or *expecting* to be kidnapped or anything remotely like that), while forgoing the usual application of zit cream (because, obviously, that would be way too embarrassing for words). Though actually, the whole acne med ban was really more for me than Sloane, since her mom keeps a highly sought-after, well-paid dermatologist on permanent retainer, just so her daughter will never have to suffer the indignity of an adolescent facial eruption.

But now, as I watch her standing there, starring in her very own cheerleading debut, I suddenly remember how my own pair of Love Pink pajamas are still all carefully folded in my bottom drawer, patiently awaiting an audience that will never show. And I wonder if it's too late to return them.

For the rest of the day, I fully committed myself to avoiding Sloane, figuring I could accomplish this by frequenting places that cheerleaders rarely go, like, for instance, the library, and the immediate area surrounding my locker. Yet wouldn't you know it, the more I went out of my way to evade her, the more it seemed like she'd multiplied. Seriously, I'm so not kidding. It was like she was *everywhere*.

Then, right before lunch, I'm in the bathroom washing my hands at the row of white porcelain sinks, when she walks in, looks right at me, and freezes like a statue.

"Congratulations," I say, forcing my face to remain as neutral as my voice, as I turn away from the sink and reach for a handful of beige paper towels.

"Thanks." She shrugs, gazing down at the ground, pressing her lips together like she always does when she's nervous.

"So, I guess that's it." I stare at her, willing her to look at me.

But she just grabs the end of her ponytail, pulls it around to the front, and starts inspecting it for imaginary split ends that I know don't exist. "I don't know what you're talking about," she finally says, shrugging for emphasis.

"*Our plan,* Sloane. You know, the one we spent the entire summer working on? The one where we swore we were in it together? The one where we promised that whoever got there first, would keep the door wide-open for the other. The one where you actually had me draft out a contract so that neither of us could default. Does that ring any bells?" I ask, narrowing my eyes and waiting for a response.

She releases her ponytail, letting it swing back and forth before settling into place, then she takes a deep breath, and says, "Listen, Winter, I know you think—"

But before she can finish, Jaci walks in. And when she sees Sloane she breaks into a huge smile and goes, "Listen well, and listen good, we're stormin' through your neighborhood!"

Followed by: clap—clap-clap—clap clap clap clap clap clap!

Oh. My. God.

Those are my *words!*

My clap sequence!

And my *cheer!*

And they *stole it!*

I stand there in shock, suddenly realizing the major role I inadvertently played in their social elevation. I mean, don't get me wrong, it's not like I think it's Pulitzer prize–winning material, but still, obviously it worked.

Then Jaci makes this high-pitched happy sound as she jumps up and down and hugs Sloane.

And Sloane hugs her back while staring at me from over her shoulder.

And me? Well, I just slam out of the bathroom and head home.

That's right, I just bail right out of there, and walk off campus, as though I don't have three more classes ahead of me. And when I get home, I head straight for my room, throw myself on my bed, and totally lose it for much longer than I care to admit.

And when I finally roll over to reach for the box of tissues my mom always puts on the table between our beds, I see the plane tickets.

And that's when I decide to go to New York.

Eight

I didn't leave a note for my mom. And I didn't call my dad. I figured I'd contact my mom once I'd safely arrived in Manhattan (so that she can cancel the Amber Alert). And my dad? Well, since I already knew how to get to both his apartment and art gallery, I figured I'd just show up at his doorstep and surprise him. And even though I realize how easy it is for a plan like that to backfire, ensuring that I'm the one who ends up getting the big surprise, the fact is, I just can't trust that he won't suddenly get all parental and tip off my mom. So you can see how I might be more than a little reluctant to RSVP.

And since I packed pretty light, have been to the city a few times before, and was unwilling to blow my admittedly meager funds on a cab ride, I bought myself a one-way Metro card and hopped on the subway, riding it all the way into SoHo, where I disembarked at the Broadway and Lafayette stop and adjusted my eyes to the darkness as I climbed the stairs into the night.

Then I trekked the few blocks to my dad's apartment, pushed the buzzer, held my breath, and hoped for the best.

But instead of saying, "Who is it?" like a normal person does when they get on the intercom, my dad goes, "Winter?"

And just like that, I know I'm in trouble.

"I think you better come up," he says, right before buzzing me in.

And by the time I get my bag and myself safely inside the vestibule, he's already on his way down to get me.

"What the hell?" he says, grabbing my stuff and shaking his head at me. I swear that's how he talks, like he's still in high school or something.

"Who told you?" I ask, following behind, unable to gauge just how much trouble I might be in.

"Autumn eventually noticed the missing ticket," he tells me, opening the door and motioning me inside. "And by the way, in case you were wondering, your mom is blaming me."

I watch as he sets my bag on the hardwood floor, then I take off my jacket and drop onto his comfortable leather couch, realizing I was so hyped-up about getting here, that I never really thought past the landing at JFK part. "Sorry," I say, gazing into his brown eyes that are just like mine, while trying to remember why I even decided to come here in the first place.

He hands me a bottle of water from the fridge behind the bar. "Does this have something to do with the tryouts?" he asks, sitting down beside me.

Oh, yeah, that. And then, like the completely uncool, total loser, retard, lame dork that I am, I drop my head in my hands and start bawling my freaking eyes out.

And when I finally calm down, having reached the point of involuntary shoulder-shaking aftershocks, he goes, "I gotta tell ya, hon, I'm a little surprised by all this. That pom-pom pep rally stuff really doesn't seem like your scene."

And when I look at him, I think, *Maybe he's right.*

I mean, even though I'd somehow convinced myself that I

really did want all that, and spent countless nights lying in bed, imagining myself all glammed out in my cheerleading garb, flirting with Cash Davis (who of course would fall madly in love with me just seconds after I'd made the squad), I'm now starting to wonder if maybe, what I actually wanted to be, was someone else.

Anyone else.

As long as I didn't have to be me.

But I don't tell him that. I just shrug and take a sip of my water.

"I should call your mom," he says, reaching for the phone. "So she'll know you got here safely. Or maybe you feel like telling her that yourself?" He looks at me, holding the receiver and waiting.

But I just shake my head, curl up on my side, and after that, I can't remember.

The next morning I wake to the sound of the front door opening, and the sight of my dad struggling with two large coffees, a bagful of bagels, and a copy of *The New York Times* for him and the *New York Post* for me.

"Here, let me help," I say, grabbing the coffees, and helping him get the table all set, smearing cream cheese across my bagel, and sipping my coffee, like this is our completely normal, everyday routine, and that I'm not really his firstborn daughter who's currently on the lam from school, not to mention life.

"So," he says, removing his black framed reading glasses, and peering at me. "What do you want to do today?"

I peek at him cautiously, wondering if this is actually for real, and if he's truly more interested in entertaining than punishing. But unable to draw any kind of conclusion, I just shrug and wait to see what he offers.

He gazes at me for a moment, then runs his hand through

his longish hair. "Well, I need to stop by the gallery for a little while, so why don't you come by around twelve, twelve-thirty? I'll show you this great installation before I take you to lunch."

Then he gets up, grabs his coffee, tosses me an extra set of keys, and heads out the door.

The second I step outside I'm glad I at least had the good sense to wear my Rock & Republic jeans. I mean, everyone around me looks so amazing and hip, and it just feels better to be wearing something that's considered universally cool.

I wander around the cobblestoned streets, looking in trendy shopwindows, and wondering if anyone other than my mom, my sister, and a few of my teachers will even notice my absence. But then I shake my head and evict that thought from my mind, remembering that phrase my mom's always going on about, "Be Here Now."

Well, I'm Here Now—in New York City. And even though I have no idea how long it'll last, I'm determined to make the most of each and every second.

By the time I make it to my dad's gallery, he's busy talking to a potential buyer. And I can tell it's a potential buyer from the way my dad is acting—displaying straight-up posture instead of his usual hipster slouch, and the way he's ditched the street slang for more proper, businesslike vernacular. Not wanting to interrupt a possible money transaction, I stroll right past him and head into the back room, looking forward to seeing his assistant, Sarah, who's been working for him for the last two years.

Only instead of Sarah, there's this drop-dead cute guy with dark curly hair, and eyes so blue I can't help but stare. Then finally I stammer, "Oh, um, I thought you were Sar— well anyway, I'll just go, and—" *Omigod!* I think, still gawking at him.

But he just smiles. "Winter, right?" He motions for me to take the seat across from his, as though it's actually his office and not my dad's.

"But, how'd you—" I start, but apparently unable to finish my sentences now, I just follow directions and take a seat in a chair that's long on style, yet painfully short on comfort.

"Your dad told me you were stopping by. I'm Easton," he says, placing his feet on the desk, and leaving me to wonder if he's just trying to get comfortable, or if I'm supposed to comment on his new, custom Converses.

"Um, who are you?" I ask.

He folds his hands behind his head and smiles. "I'm the intern. I get school credit for working here a couple hours a week."

"Serious?" I say, thinking how I'd love to enroll in a cool school like that.

"I go to one of those art schools, you know, for actors and musicians and stuff."

"Like the *Fame* school?" I ask, not that I've actually seen *Fame,* but I know that's what everyone calls those kinds of schools.

He smiles, which gets me feeling so nervous again my eyes dart around the office in order to avoid his.

And just as I'm racking my brain, trying to think of something to say that won't sound totally stupid and out me as the consummate geek that I truly am, my dad pokes his head in and goes, "Ready?"

So I reach for my purse and head for the door, and just as I turn back toward Easton, he smiles and winks.

And that gets me so off-balance I walk smack into the doorjamb. The toe of my boot crashing into it so hard it makes this awful loud *thud,* as the rest of my body moves forward, stopping only when the tip of my nose is all out of give and smashed down to the bone. Like an anxious pug, straining against a car window. Only not near as cute.

But even though I'm totally and completely humiliated, not to mention how my nose really does kind of hurt, I still force myself to laugh and say, "I'm okay, I'm okay." Long before anyone can ask.

Then I follow my dad out of the gallery and onto the street, tenderly touching the bridge of my nose, checking for swelling and hoping it's not broken.

Somewhere between the french fries and the French onion soup, my dad looks at me and goes, "So, what exactly are we doing here?"

And I think, *here it is, the moment of truth.* I mean, I knew it would come sooner or later, but excuse me for hoping for later.

I just shrug, and dip a *frite* into my soup, determined not to make this any easier for him.

He rests his forearms on the table, leans toward me, and says, "The way I see it, you got two choices."

Oh, great. I gaze up at him.

"One, you go back tomorrow, confront your demons, and get on with your life." He looks right at me.

"And two?" I ask, hoping for a better option, but fearing it could be even worse.

"Two, you finish out the week with me, and head back this weekend, well rested and ready to confront your demons on Monday."

I let out a deep breath and smile. "You know, I haven't actually told you this, but my demon has a name," I say, looking right at him.

But he just laughs. "Let me guess, Sloane?" He sips his wine and raises his eyebrows.

"How'd you know?" I ask, my eyes going wide, wondering for a fleeting moment if maybe he's psychic.

But he just shrugs. "Lucky guess."

After just a few days in the city, I was so entrenched in my new life of leisure, no responsibility, and zero peer pressure, that I was starting to fantasize about making it permanent. I mean, if you think about it, why couldn't it work? I loved my dad, he loved me, and it's not like I had anything to miss back home. Okay, maybe I'd miss my mom, and maybe even Autumn if I were gone long enough. But since I hadn't been gone long enough yet, it was kind of hard to imagine.

It's like, I was spending my days strolling through Central Park, going to museums and galleries with my dad, eating at some of the hippest restaurants in town, and had even done some mad shopping with a wad of cash he'd given me.

"Go crazy," he'd said, and believe me, I did. Buying up all kinds of cool stuff, like dark denim stovepipe jeans, this amazing black bubble hem dress, a black leather purse with fringe and silver studs stuck all over it, leggings, tunics, ankle boots, and all kinds of other hip stuff that, believe me, Sloane and her pastel posse would never go near. But now that I wasn't going to be one of them, I was thinking that maybe I could just try to be me. Or at least the me that I wanted to be.

Not to mention how despite the whole nose-smacking incident, I seemed to have this growing (and very promising) flirtation with Easton. I mean, I'd started dropping by the gallery whenever I knew he'd be there, and we'd hang out in the back office and laugh and talk and drink strong, bitter coffee out of those little blue paper cups with the Greek key design that just scream *New York!* And it is so cool to hang with him, and not just because he's so amazingly cute (which he is!), but also because he's just so much smarter and so much more interesting than all the guys who go to my school put together. Seriously. It's like, he actually knows stuff about art, and literature, and theater, and film, and restaurants, and clubs, and world travel, not to mention how he's been a working actor ever since he was a little kid and scored his first diaper commercial.

I mean, even though I know most kids think Laguna Beach is like the coolest place on the planet because of that MTV show and all, trust me, I've lived there my whole entire life, and the world they depict on that show has nothing to do with mine.

So on Friday, I was on my way to the gallery for this big-deal reception my dad was throwing for a "very promising young artist." Some grad-school chick named Angley Hayes, who did a group of self-portraits that apparently people are already buzzing about. And even though I can't really vouch for how "promising" she might be, I will say this: there's nothing quite like staring at a row of wall-sized, full frontal, awkwardly posed, anatomically correct nudes with your dad on one side and the artist on the other.

But by the time I get there, I can hardly believe how packed this place is. I mean, I wasn't really sure what an art reception would actually be like, but it's more like a party than I thought. There's like a huge crowd of superhip, artsy-looking people, standing around with drinks and little plates of hors d'oeuvres, while some really great, yet unidentifiable (at least to me) music pumps in the background.

So I'm walking around, scanning the room for my dad and Easton (though not necessarily in that order), and just as I spot my dad across the room talking to some disturbingly pretty model type, I hear someone say, "Hey."

And I turn and look right into those amazing blue eyes. "Hey," I say, taking the glass that Easton's offering and trying to act all cool and casual, even though my knees are about to buckle and my heart is pumping like crazy. I mean, he's wearing a white T-shirt, a suede blazer, designer jeans, cool shoes, and with his hair kind of wild and curly around his face, he looks totally and completely irresistible.

"It's just club soda." He shrugs, taking a sip of his. "I'll try to score something better when your dad gets too busy to notice." He smiles.

And even though I'm not quite sure how I feel about his plan to take advantage of my dad's inattention, I just nod and smile, too.

"Listen, I'm planning to cut out pretty soon, and meet up with some people, and I was wondering if maybe you'd want to come along?" he asks, peering at me from over the top of his cup, waiting for a response.

Do I wanna come along? Is he kidding? But then I gaze across the room at my dad, my shoulders sinking when I realize I'll have to clear it with him first.

"Go ahead, ask your old man." Easton nods. "I'm sure he won't mind."

Then he smiles at me, and I smile at him, and when I gaze at my dad, I hope that it's true.

"So, where we going?" I ask, walking beside him, and wondering if this could actually be considered a date. I mean, not that I've ever been on one before, but it seems like all of the symptoms are present and accounted for. Like, I'm going to a party with this amazingly cute guy, who, believe it or not, actually wants to be with me. So it seems like that should definitely count, right?

"Friend of mine's having a little gathering, I thought we'd stop by and check it out," he says, before leading me into this really modern-looking building that houses the most amazing loft I've ever seen (and that includes TV, movies, and pictures in magazines).

I gaze around at the floor-to-ceiling windows, the walls covered in large, abstract, original works of art, and a roomful of kids so cool and beautiful I feel like I've stepped into a *Teen Vogue* photo shoot. Then I gaze down at my new, black, bubble hem dress and hope that it's really as cool as I think.

"Come on," Easton says, grabbing my hand and leading me into the designated den area. "Let me introduce you around."

Okay, so here's the short list of things I've never done before:

1. Gone to a party with a hot guy.
2. Gone to a party where there were no adult chaperones.
3. Sipped anything stronger than a double espresso.
4. Kissed a guy as cute as Easton. (Or any guy for that matter.)

And if things went well, I was hoping tonight I could start a new list.

So, I'm sitting on this really low, supermodern, circular sofa, and Easton is so close to me that his leg is actually overlapping on mine (which, believe me, is pretty much all I can think about). And I'm just sitting there like Switzerland (you know, all neutral), while Easton gets in this heated debate with some guy called Gin (though I'm not sure why, since Gin is actually drinking a beer) about some book that I've never even read, much less heard of. Which is pretty amazing when I think about all the books I've devoured. And as I listen to them argue back and forth, I'm starting to realize that not only are these kids cooler than me, richer than me, more beautiful than me, more informed than me, but apparently, they're also way smarter than me.

"Anyway, books are irrelevant. The twenty-first century is all about blogging," Gin says, shaking his head and sipping Pilsner Urquell straight from the bottle.

But apparently, Easton's not buying it, since he rolls his eyes, and goes, "Bullshit. Blogging's just a bunch of assholes with a keyboard and an opinion. Hyped-up fare that works hard at blurring the boundaries between actual news and completely biased perspective. And, at its very worst, it's just more rumor-mongering tabloid crap." He shakes his head and sips from his red plastic party cup.

I just sit there, sipping my drink, but not saying a word. Partly because I can't risk having them think I'm stupid by opening my mouth and removing all doubt, and partly because I cannot believe that people my age actually *talk like this*. I mean, I've been sitting here for what surely must be at least a half hour now, and already they've touched on the war in Iraq, the likelihood of the first female president and who it will be, and have now moved on to Big Media. I mean, don't these people realize that Jessica left Nick, Brad ditched Jen, and Paris will no longer speak to Nicole?

"That's the point. It's all about perspective, which is the same thing any writer does. Except with blogging you get the immediate gratification of making your views instantly available, in real time, for free."

Immediate gratification . . . that's what I need, I think, taking two quick, yet substantial, sips of my Bacardi and Coke. I mean, I like to write, so maybe I should start a blog. I could write about being a lunchtime loser and call it, "The View from Table C." Or I could write about life in the It town for the non-It girl and call it, "Laguna Beach: The Painfully Real O. C."

"That's total crap! Blogs will never replace the novel. Because in the end, people still want their tactile experience. You cannot curl up in front of a nice roaring fire, with a cup of hot cocoa, and your shiny, cold, Apple iBook. It's just not the same experience," Easton says, shaking his head and finishing his drink, as Gin, the heated debater, just laughs and walks away.

I look at Easton and think how I could really get used to living like this. You know, hanging out in other people's amazing lofts, with a group of young, cool, smart people who talk about interesting things, and where I'd enjoy an exciting, hip life that I could totally blog about in my spare time. Let's face it, it definitely beats the sad and empty lunch table I've got waiting for me back home.

"What're you thinking?" Easton asks, leaning toward me, looking at me in a way that I originally thought I wanted him to, only now I'm not so sure.

"Um, nothing," I say, shrugging nervously, not quite willing to share my latest New York blogger fantasy with him.

Then he slides his hand into his pocket, pulls it back out, and opens his palm. And as I stare at the medium-sized joint, just lying there in his hand, I realize I've just added a fifth to my list.

I watch as he grabs a small box of matches, lights up the end, and takes a substantial drag before passing it to me. And as I hold it between my fingers, I think about how, for pretty much the last five years of my life, everyone from school administrators with their awkward auditorium talks, to TV celebrities starring in public service announcements, to even my very own, well-meaning (yet ultimately hypocritical if you count those brownies they used to bake that Autumn and I weren't, under any circumstances, ever allowed to eat) parents, have been doing their best to coach me for just this very moment. And even though their advice was all slightly different, the message behind it was always the same—*just* don't *do it!* Like the world's most negative Nike ad.

So it's not like I haven't been well versed and overrehearsed in how I'm supposed to handle such a moment. I mean, over and over again I've been told to just smile demurely, shake my head, and take a pass. But even after knowing all that, despite all that well-meaning antidrug message-mongering, I still place it right between my lips as I proceed to mimic every single thing I saw Easton just do.

Only I don't really inhale.

In fact, I don't inhale at all. I just totally fake like I did, and then I shyly turn away from him, so that I can politely release a fake cloud of invisible, nonexistent, imaginary smoke. But as I pass it back, I make sure to cough just a little, so everything will appear completely legit, so he'll never guess that I'm a virgin.

After he takes a few more hits, I take one final fake one, then he stubs it out, drops it into a heavy crystal ashtray, leans in, and starts kissing me. And even though I admit that I've never actually done this before either, there's just no way I'm faking it. So I lean in, too, wrapping my arms around his neck, and concentrating on kissing him back, just like I practiced on my hand for the last three years, hoping I'm pulling this off even half as well as I did with the whole pot-smoking thing.

And even though it's not nearly as romantic as I'd expected, and even though there's absolutely no trace of that completely swoony feeling I was sure I would experience if I was ever lucky enough to kiss a guy as hot as Easton, that doesn't mean it's not nice. But just when I think I'm really getting the hang of it, he pulls away, grabs both our cups, and heads for the bar to make a refill run. While I remain on the couch, feeling simultaneously dazed and elated, thinking how I can't wait to share that with Sloane.

But then I remember how I can't exactly do that anymore, since we're no longer friends. And how that's pretty much the reason why I came here in the first place.

So then I gaze around the room at all these amazing people with names like India Pink and Calla Lily (which definitely makes me feel better about my own weird name), and I think, *Screw Sloane.* And screw those stupid, superficial, synthetic cheerleader clones too. I mean, they may be cool in their zip code, but in this one? Not so much.

And when Easton returns and hands me my drink, I take a sip, smiling when I realize I can now start a new list.

I'm not sure how it happened, but somehow Easton is on top of me, kissing the side of my neck and moving his hips in a way that simulates something I've definitely never done before. And when I turn my head to the side, I open my eyes, and peer all around, and from what I can see in this dim, shadowy light, we're definitely not the only ones doing this.

So I focus back on Easton, trying to concentrate on just kissing him, but my head feels so weird, and my brain feels so soggy, then all of a sudden the whole room starts spinning around and around like when you're on that Mad Tea Party ride at Disneyland. So I squeeze my eyes shut, and make my body go all stiff, hoping that will somehow slow it all down, or even make it stop. And then I feel Easton's hand creeping its way inside the top part of my dress, and even though I'd already decided I'd *maybe* let him do that if he tried, now that it's actually happening, I'm thinking maybe not.

And then, *oh, my God,* I feel that sudden, unmistakable, unstoppable urge to vomit. And I know I have like maybe ten seconds to get out of here before I blow.

Frantically, I push Easton off, so hard that he falls to the floor and goes, "Hey!" Then I get up and bolt for the door, crushing a few stray limbs along the way, but with no time to apologize.

Then with my hand clamped firmly over my mouth, knowing that I cannot, under any circumstances, projectile vomit anywhere inside this trillion-dollar loft, I head straight through the door and onto the street where it's all fair game. And I lean into some bushes and just stay like that, heaving and puking 'til there's nothing left.

When I'm finally empty, I just stand there, all hunched over, wiping my mouth with the back of my hand, feeling helpless, shaky, and humiliated as hell. And then Easton arrives with my purse in his hand, going, "Are you okay?" While looking at me with so much concern, it makes me feel even worse.

I just nod, even though I think it's probably pretty obvious that I'm not.

And he says, "Here, let me take you home."

But I shake my head and avoid his eyes. "Just get me a cab," I mumble, gazing down at the ground, amazed at how the trip from "cool" to "loser" was a lot quicker than I would've thought.

He hails a taxi, and gets me safely inside, and when he closes the door between us, he goes, "Uh, you're not gonna mention any of this to your dad, are you?"

But the cab pulls away from the curb before I can answer.

Nine

Even though I didn't exactly tell my dad, it's not like he didn't know. I mean, remember the band, the Billboard hit, and the whole rock star thing? Well, trust me, I couldn't have fooled him if I tried.

So the next morning, by the time I finally make it into the kitchen, there's a big bottle of water along with two extra-strength aspirins, waiting patiently beside my coffee.

"So how bad was it?" he asks, peering at me from over the top of his folded in half newspaper.

But I just shrug, and drop my head in my hands. Because even though I have no other hangover stories to judge it by, I'm definitely convinced that it's probably pretty bad.

"Should I have stopped you?" he asks, gazing at me with concern.

I swear that's how he parents. Like everything is this thoroughly considered, nonpartisan, fairly voted on, democratic decision. And when it doesn't work out? Well, that's when it becomes "a learning experience." So obviously, it's pretty tough to get in trouble around here.

I just look at him and shrug. "In retrospect? Maybe," I tell him.

But he just laughs. "So?" He looks at me, waiting for all the dirty details.

Oh, yeah, that's the other part of his parenting, he likes to be kept well-informed and in the loop. So full disclosure is the price you pay for not being put on restriction.

"Two Bacardi and Cokes, half a beer, and like, two or three pretend hits of pot," I confess. "But that's it. Scout's honor," I say, raising my right hand as though I'm solemnly swearing.

He just looks at me, eyebrows raised.

"What can I say? You raised a lightweight." I shrug. "Oh, yeah, and then I deposited all of it in the bushes right outside of the most amazing loft you've ever seen."

"You're way better off, trust me," he says, nodding his head while taking a swig of iced coffee.

"Funny, I don't feel better off." I shrug. "I mean, I have red eyes, dry mouth, a raging headache, a bad case of embarrassment, a world of regret, and a pretty heavy dose of much humbled humiliation."

"And Easton?" He looks at me, waiting.

"He's totally terrified that I'll tell you," I say, swallowing the aspirin, followed by a hearty chug of mineral water chaser.

"And did you learn anything?" he asks, still looking at me.

"Believe me, I learned plenty," I assure him, grabbing the *New York Post* and searching for Page Six.

The rest of the day was pretty low-key. Partly because of my delicate condition, and partly because it was our last day together so we just wanted to be mellow. So after taking a leisurely stroll through the park, we went to a matinee, and then headed to one of my dad's favorite haunts to enjoy an early dinner. And even though I was still fending off a few residual shakes, I was mostly just thinking about how great it was to hang with my dad, one-on-one for a change, and not have to share him with Autumn, or one of his many girlfriends.

"How come you never got remarried?" I ask, taking a bite of the hamburger he made me order (swearing that the mixture of protein and grease would be good for my queasy stomach), while glaring at the back of the waitress's head, the one who spent the last twenty minutes flirting with my dad, auditioning for the role of my new mommy.

"I don't think I'm cut out for it," he says, sipping his chardonnay and looking at me.

"That's exactly what Mom says," I tell him, as he sets down his glass and smiles.

"Speaking of, are you ready to face the music?" he asks, eyebrows raised.

"Do I have to?" I hold my breath.

"No. But I think you should."

I took at him for a moment, and then I just nod, dragging my french fry through a puddle of ketchup, knowing he's right.

The second we get back to the apartment, Easton calls. I guess he wanted to make peace with my dad, make sure he's not fired, and say good-bye to me (yes, in that order). And after my dad gave him a lecture so severe it left me with my mouth hanging open in shock, he handed me the phone, and promptly left the room.

"Hey," I say, plopping onto the couch, kicking off my shoes, and resting my bare feet on the coffee table.

"So, your dad seems pretty upset," he says, sounding kind of scared and nervous, and not at all like the overconfident guy from last night.

"Yeah, well." I just shrug, and gaze at my pedicure that's in desperate need of revision.

"Okay, well, I just wanted to say that it was really cool meeting you."

"Yeah, you too," I say, feeling relieved that he's not completely turned-off and grossed-out by the whole puking fiasco.

"So, when do you think you'll be back?" he asks.

"No idea," I tell him. "Probably not 'til summer though."

"Okay, well, next time you're in the city, you should definitely look me up," he says, sounding cool and casual, and maybe, just maybe, even a little bit hopeful.

And after I agree to "definitely" do that, I lean against the cushions, close my eyes, and replay my incredible week in New York. It's like, in the course of just five days, I grew closer to my dad, hung out in the coolest city in the world, added some crucial pieces to my wardrobe, knocked five items off of my "virgin list," and (most important of all) survived my first romance-hook up quickie boyfriend pretty much unscathed.

And even though all of those things originally had me longing to stay, I now know that because of them, I'm finally ready to go.

Ten

Jeez, you'd think I'd been gone a month the way my mom and Autumn hugged me at the airport. Though to be honest, I actually kind of missed them, too. And the first thing I do when we get back home is head for my room, then I freeze in the doorway, dropping my bag in shock, when I see how everything has changed. And I don't mean that I've been gone so long that I now see everything in a fresh, new light kind of changed. I mean that, literally, *everything has changed*. There are new dressers, new beds, new sheets, there's even these cool new curtains that surround each of our beds, so that Autumn and I can share a room without having to constantly look at each other.

"So what do you think?" my mom asks, as Autumn stands beside her, smiling.

"I love it!" I gaze all around, touching the soft cotton curtain, and running my hand over my cool, new dresser drawers. Then I look at them, and they're so excited about the fact that

I'm excited, that it makes me feel horrible for running away like that. "I'm sorry I ran off," I say. "I just—"

But my mom raises her hand and shakes her head, sign language for "it's my turn to talk." "Believe me, I've thought long and hard about this, Winter, and while I realize you're growing up and that we may not always see eye to eye, I'm afraid I can't just let this one go. You know there are consequences to your actions."

I stare at her, my stomach heading south while I wonder what she could possibly have in mind. *Damn, I knew all the hugs and furniture were too good to be true.*

"I went along with the cheerleading, haven't said a word about your new hair color, and the other day I actually left the store early so I could drive you to the mall. And even though I may disapprove of some of your more recent choices, I haven't tried to stop you because I know they're important to you. But this, running off to New York without so much as a note." She shakes her head. "Well, you have no idea how worried I was. So for the next two weeks, I want you coming straight home from school, no detours, no side trips, and no TV. You missed a lot of schoolwork and I want you fully caught up. I also want to know that I can trust you again."

She raises her eyebrows and lowers her chin, as I exhale slowly and nod. I mean, what else can I do? I'm getting off easy. And trying to barter her down will only backfire.

By dinnertime, all anyone can talk about is Rey. Seriously, all through the salad and well into the main course, it's like "Rey this," and "Rey that." And, "Oh, my God, remember that time when Rey said such and such?"

So finally, I bite. "Okay, who the heck is Rey?" I ask, twirling my pasta onto my spoon and glancing from my mom to Autumn.

"This young boy I hired last week," my mom says, taking a small sip of her sparkling water with lime.

And since my mom's definition of "young boy" pretty much covers anyone between the ages of three and thirty, I say, "Details, please." Then I take a bite of pasta so big I need a pair of scissors to cut it, just like on that old episode of "I Love Lucy."

"He's sixteen, just moved to Laguna, and he's taking over your shift at the café," she informs me.

"My shift?" I stare at her. "But why? I was gone less than a week, and you already replaced me?" I mean, jeez, just because I sometimes complain about having to work there doesn't mean I actually wanted to stop. Especially now that my life's so lonely and pathetic I have no other way of filling up all my spare time.

But my mom just looks at me carefully, obviously confused by my reaction. Then she says in a soft, patient voice, "Well, honey, when you ran off like that, I thought all the pressure was getting to be too much for you, and that maybe you'd enjoy having your weekends off, you know, to spend more time with your friends. So I hired Rey to pick up the slack."

I just glare at her. I mean, *hello*? Now that Sloane has gone to the other side I'm pretty much all out of friends. And even though I realize how my mom can't possibly know any of that (since I haven't exactly divulged any of it), I can't help being upset. I mean, I feel like she should just *know*.

"I'm sorry, I thought you'd be happy," she says, giving me a worried look. "Because now you can spend all of your Friday and Saturday nights with Sloane."

And just like *that* I feel like I never even left. Like I'm picking up exactly where I left off, and that nothing has changed, least of all me. "Yeah, well that's just great, Mom," I say, shaking my head, dangerously close to tears. "Except for the fact that Sloane and I aren't exactly friends anymore, and somehow I just completely forgot to cast an understudy."

I push away from the table and my still half full plate of

food, and make a run for my room, where I close the door, grab the laptop I share with Autumn, and pull my cool new privacy curtain until it's secured all around me. And then, just to torture myself even more, I check my e-mail, which just makes me feel worse when I realize that my twelve new messages are what most people call spam. And since I'm not currently interested in stock market investing, penile enhancement, or Viagra, I delete every last one, until my screen is finally clear and my in-box shows 0.

Then I sit there, just staring at that sad empty number, thinking how nice it would be to have a constantly ringing phone and a *legitimately* full in-box, yet painfully aware of how I haven't the slightest idea how to actually go about getting any of that. I mean, I'm actually pretty shy, which is like a major handicap when it comes to making new friends.

But what if I were to start a blog, or live journal, or whatever they call those things?

What if I created my own Web space where I could write about something interesting, yet in a totally anonymous way? I wouldn't even have to use my real name. Heck, I wouldn't even have to say where I live. I could just simply create this whole new persona, one that's smart, cool, and engaging. One that people would actually want to read about, talk about, and maybe even contact. I mean, just because I lack an interesting life, doesn't mean I lack an interesting opinion.

And then before I can really stop and think it over, before I can make one of my usual pro/con lists, I'm all signed up and signed in with my very own blog. I've even managed to come up with a really good, really secure screen name that will totally shield my identity, yet still has a unique and personal meaning to me. I'm calling myself Eleanor Rigby. After an old Beatles song about all these lonely people that my mom always played when I was a kid.

So, feeling all excited about my new identity, I stare for a moment at that intimidating, blank screen, then I type:

Sunday, September ??, 2006

7:45 P.M.

Current Mood—been better

Current Music—"Town Called Malice" by the Jam

                (well, it's playing in my head anyway)

Quote of the Day—Um, coming soon

Under Construction—Check Back Soon

Okay, so as far as blogging goes, I guess I'm off to a pretty dismal start. I mean, just because I found a name for my new persona, doesn't mean I have the backstory to go with it. But it will come. I know it will. I just have to be patient.

They weren't kidding about the ton of homework. So by lunch when I find myself so loaded down with make-up assignments and chapters to read that I have no idea how I'll ever catch up, I decide to just go to the library and get a head start. Not to mention how this will also keep me from having to eat lunch at the lonely, desolate Table C, as well as lower my risk of running into Sloane again. I mean, I'm just four periods and one ten-minute break into the day and I've already seen her three times. And even though I know I've got three full years of Sloane sightings ahead of me, at the moment, I'm determined to take it just one period at a time.

But do you think she said hi? Or did anything remotely polite in honor of our eight years of friendship? Nope. She just averted her eyes and carried on with her new friends, acting like she didn't even see me.

Like I wasn't even there.

Like I was invisible to her too now.

So I try to make myself feel better by remembering how just a few nights ago I was making out in a loft, in Manhattan, with a totally hot actor guy (while somehow omitting the other less attractive parts of that story). And I smile when I realize how Sloane, cool as she may be these days, has yet to do anything remotely as cool as that.

And then, just as I turn the corner, I'm suddenly confronted with a sight so horrible, and so freaking unbelievable, that I'm unable to do anything other than stop and stare.

Because standing right there, no more than twenty feet away, are Sloane and Ginny. And standing right alongside them? Well, that would be none other than Andy Spence and Cash Davis.

And not only is Cash standing next to Sloane, but he's also smiling.

And not only is he smiling, but he's also talking.

And I stand there watching as everyone laughs at whatever incredibly clever thing he just said, noticing how Sloane puts some major extra effort into her laugh. Throwing her head back, so that her long, blond hair swings brilliantly from side to side, while clutching herself in a way that emphasizes her maximum waist-to-hip ratio. And while she's busy engaging in this bit of well-rehearsed, painstakingly choreographed, primitive flirtation ritual, I watch as Cash moves in even closer, as though he wants nothing more in this world than to hold her hand, brush her hair, or make out with her, or something.

And the sight of all *this,* the realization that she's actually well on her way to getting *everything* we both always wanted, that her application has been approved and she is now free to partake in all the perks of membership (while I'm left standing on the sidelines, like last year's It bag), makes me feel so unbelievably sick, nauseous, and grief-stricken, that I spin around and run blindly toward the library, where I smack right into some weirdo with a guitar.

"Hey, there!" he says, regaining his balance, as I look at him with eyes so wild and teary he actually appears blurry to me.

"Hey, are you okay?" His voice softer now, as he leans in for a closer look.

"I'm fine," I say, glancing at him only briefly, but still long enough to take in his straight dark choppy hair; brown heavily lashed eyes; kinda pale skin; long, lean, lanky build; shiny black dress shoes; slim-fitting black dress pants; crisp white dress shirt; black skinny tie; ultra-tailored black blazer; and of course, that ridiculous guitar. The only things missing are a

British accent, a Vespa, and the Who's *Quadrophenia* soundtrack. I mean where does he think he is? 1980?

"Yeah, well, you don't look all that fine," he says, still peering at me with concern.

"Excuse me?" I stare at him. *I mean, did he really just say that?*

But then his face turns all red and he looks all embarrassed when he goes, "No! What I meant was you look good. Really good. But you also look kind of upset, that's all."

But I'm in no mood for this. I mean, my stomach hurts, my eyes are stinging, my throat aches, and all I want is to get far away from him, far away from everybody, so that I can find a nice corner, hunker down, and try to figure out how on earth I became such a big, embarrassing loser. So I just look at him and go, "Okay, are we done here? 'Cause I really need to get to the library."

And I watch as he bows down before me, swinging his arm and sending me on my way, like he's about to say "As you wish, milady," like we're on the set of *Pride and Prejudice* or something.

But I just shake my head, roll my eyes, and walk away. Thinking how typical it is that the only person who's talked to me this entire day is an even bigger freak than me.

By the time I make it to my seventh-period chemistry class, guess who I find occupying the stool directly across from mine? That's right, Mr. Guitar Geek himself.

"Greetings," he says, as I slide onto my stool, dropping my backpack hard on the table. "Are you new here?"

But I just grab my notebook, flip it open, and go searching for my favorite pen. "Trust me, you're the one who's new here," I say, setting it next to my notebook and barely glancing at him.

"Well, since I was here last week, and this is the first I've seen of you, I beg to differ." He gives me an amused look.

"Beg all you want, but I was out of town." I shrug, looking away again so I won't have to look at him.

"Oh, really? Now was this for business or pleasure?" he asks, cupping his chin in his hand and leaning toward me like he really is interested.

But I'm not divulging any details. And to be honest, even though he seems nice enough (well, despite all the weirdness), I'm really not feeling all that up for this. So I just shake my head and gaze at the chalkboard, watching as my teacher covers it with formulas, which after missing just a few days of school, I can no longer understand.

Eleven

The next day I'm standing at the counter in Dietrich's, ordering a coffee and a cookie and just basically minding my own
business, when someone sneaks up from behind, leans toward
my ear, and starts singing, "Glance around, sky is brown, and
the ground, is a crazy shade of winter."

And when I turn, I come face-to-face with weirdo guitar
guy who's standing there with a big smile spread all across his
face. "It's *hazy* shade of winter." I roll my eyes and shake my
head. "And by the way, you flubbed all the other lyrics, too," I
inform him, even though I'm actually pretty surprised by his
nice, clear, melodic voice.

"I know." He smiles. "But how did *you* know?"

"My mom raised me on the Simon and Garfunkel version,
even though it took the Bangles to really rock it on the *Less
Than Zero* soundtrack back in the eighties. But since my mom
won't listen to anything recorded after summer 1979, it's not
like she even knows about that version," I say, wondering why

I just divulged all that useless, nonsense information, like the second after it's out and way too late to take it back.

"Hated the movie. Liked the book." He smiles.

"So, how'd you know my name?" I ask, grabbing my coffee and moving away from the counter.

"Your mom told me."

I squint at him, wondering if he could possibly be serious. *I mean, hello? How creepy is this?*

"I'm Rey," he says, extending his hand.

"Oh, but of course, my mom's favorite new adopted son," I say, heading for a seat at my usual table. "Believe me, I know all about you, you love classic rock, organic foods, and care deeply about the environment. And now, apparently, you're stalking me." I watch as he grabs the seat across from mine. "Or is following me around and spying on me part of your job description? 'Cause I gotta warn ya, it's gonna get *pretty* boring." I take a sip of my coffee, and wait for him to respond.

But he just smiles.

"So tell me, how'd you know it was me? Did she show you all of my baby pictures, make you watch old home movies with your eyelids clipped open *Clockwork Orange*–style, so you wouldn't doze off?" I ask, thinking how I wouldn't put it past her.

But he just laughs. "Nope, though I'd love to see some of those old photos when you get a chance. Actually, I'm the one who helped her distribute all the missing person posters and organize that press conference when you disappeared. Of course, all that took place well before we realized you were hiding out in New York. How'd that go by the way? You seem pretty mum on the whole subject."

I just roll my eyes and take a bite of my white chocolate chunk macadamia nut cookie. "Are you planning to tell her about this?" I ask, pointing at the cookie, evidence of my most egregious crime so far today. "That I make it a point to regularly consume products crammed with empty calories and saturated fat when she's not around?"

But he just smiles and reaches over to break off a piece for himself. "Wouldn't dream of it," he says.

So, apparently, not only do I have a new morning coffee partner, a new ten-minute-break partner, a new lab partner, but I also seem to have a new lunch partner. Not that I asked for it, and not that I even want it, not to mention how I wish he'd just dump that lame guitar already, since I've heard like a ton of people make fun of it. But it's not like he cares.

"I can't worry about shit like that," he says, when I mention how he might want to consider leaving it at home, preferably in the back of his closet, behind the black trench coat I'm sure that he owns. "I've been to more schools than I can count, and it's all the same. Not one of them stands out as special or different. Though try telling them that." He shakes his head, which causes a chunk of long, dark brown bang to fall over his right eye. "Like those girls over there," he says, pointing at Jaci, Holly, Claire, and Sloane. "I bet I can tell you everything about them, even though I've never even seen them before today."

I just roll my eyes, and take another bite of my sandwich.

"You don't believe me?" he asks, eyebrows raised. "Fine, here goes. The blonde in the center?" He points at Jaci, and looks briefly at me. "She's in charge. And the one standing right there to her left, she's second in line. She's the one who'll take over in the event that the queen can no longer fulfill her royal duties. And, by the way, they all like the same guy, which, from what I can see is probably that one standing right over there." He points at Cash. "Because everything they're doing, all the laughing, and hair tossing? It's just the same old tired attempt to get his attention. And as long as it stays theoretical it'll all be fine. But the second one of them actually hooks up with him, stand back, because the claws will come out and it'll be all-out war." He sneaks a peek at me and continues. "Let's see, they all like the same stupid, vacuous movies, only read books if they have to, secretly wish they were Hilary Duff, and consult with one another every morning before school for outfit approval. Have you heard enough, or should I move on to the jocks and really dazzle you with my insight?" He smiles.

But I just drop my sandwich and shake my head. "The one on the right? The one who you said was poised to take over?" I look at him. "Up until two weeks ago she was my best and only friend in the whole wide world," I say, feeling my throat go all tight, and my eyes sting with tears, as I wonder why on earth I just divulged all that.

But Rey just looks at me and smiles. "Looks like you got out just in time," he says.

After school, I go to my room, get on the computer, and check out Rey's Web site that he told me about. And I'm not talking about some typical MySpace page where he talks about his lame hobbies, lists brand names under "major interests," and forces you to listen to some song you don't even like. I mean he has a *real* Web site, with a real Web address, and photos, art-work, song lyrics (all original, all his), multiple pages to browse through, interesting things to read, and all kinds of links to all kinds of other cool stuff.

And the thing is, the more I read about him, the worse I feel. I mean, Rey's actually a pretty interesting guy, and he really has lived all over the place, including long stints in both London and Madrid. But the reason I feel so bad is because reading all this stuff is making it clear how I've been so busy talking about myself and Sloane and Table A, that I haven't really shown much interest in him. I mean, hello? No wonder I don't have any friends.

But from what I've read so far, I now know that he was in a band when he lived in New York. Which from what I can see was actually his last address, and apparently they used to play in all these clubs and stuff even though he's only like sixteen and technically not even old enough to go in a club. So then, of course, I start wondering if maybe he knows Easton, even though I know how that probably seems kind of lame since there's like millions of other people who live in Manhattan and go to clubs, too. But still, you just never know. So while part of me is thinking about asking him, the other part is already pretty sure that I won't. I mean, I'd kind of like to keep all of that private, and only for me. So that I can always remember it *my* way, and not run the risk of compromising my memory by having Rey give me the whole analytical rundown on Easton, too.

And while I'm tooling around his Web site, learning all the little details of his life, reading his song lyrics, and checking out his artwork, I notice that he also has a blog link. So I click on that, and start skim-reading some entries, feeling pretty impressed not only by how good it is, but how he actually seemed to utilize spell check. I mean, let's face it, it's an impatient world, and most people don't even bother.

But since his stuff reads more like a review than a journal, giving his opinions on stuff like politics, music, art, and books, it doesn't exactly help me with mine. I mean, even though I still have no idea what to write, I know I'm not really informed enough to write like that.

The next day at school, all I can think about is my blog. Which I know probably sounds a little strange since I haven't actually posted anything on it yet, but after waking at 4:15 with the sudden inspiration of a great new idea, I haven't been able to think about anything else. I mean, I was so excited that I actually considered grabbing the computer and signing on right then, but since I couldn't risk waking Autumn, I forced my way back to sleep, assuring myself that I'd get to it later

But now that I have a subject, now that I have a pretty clear idea what I'm going to write, I also have this whole new perspective on school. And suddenly, strolling through campus and seeing Sloane practically everywhere I go is no longer the nightmare it used to be. Because now, every time I see Sloane talking with Ginny, fake-hugging Jaci, or tossing her hair and flirting with Cash, it no longer eats me in the way that it used to. Now, I just stop and take it all in, making notes in my head, and saving it for later, because it's all just juice for the blog.

And I feel so empowered just knowing that every time she snubs me she's actually given me something to write about, that I can finally wander the campus in peace, drifting in and out of classrooms, while filling the page in my head, adding to it, editing it down, and rearranging paragraphs, until I can hardly wait to get home and do it for real.

"So what do you say?" Rey asks, leaning on the lunch table and looking at me.

I turn to face him. "Sorry, what?"

"I was asking if you wanted to check out this band on Friday. They do this amazing rendition of 'Gobsmacked.' I swear, it's so good, you've got to hear it."

"That's my dad's song," I mumble, turning back toward Sloane (who, by the way, has just now made her way to the top of Table A), watching as she tosses her long, shiny blond hair (just like she practiced in front of her mirror all last summer), while her hands wave all around, rehearsing some of her cheerleading moves. And believe me, even though I know that I'm staring, and that staring is considered to be universally rude (right up there with finger-pointing and flipping the bird), it's not like I feel the least bit bad about it. Because:

1. It's research.
2. I'm only giving her what she wants.

I mean, why sit on top of something if you don't want everyone to look at you?

But apparently Rey's still stuck on this whole "Gobsmacked" business, because he goes, "Excuse me? Did you just say that's your dad's song?" Then he reaches across the table and grabs my arm.

But I just nod because I'm busy watching Sloane pretend that she totally hates it when Cash picks her up, throws her over his shoulder (yes, you can see her underwear, but since she's wearing those thick, opaque, cheerleader modesty bloomer things I don't think it really counts), and acts like he's going to drag her back to his cave or something. And when he finally puts her back down, she takes full advantage of the opportunity to fluff up her hair so that it falls all loose and wild around her shoulders, before fake-punching him in the arm and breaking into perfectly timed, yet totally insincere, squeals of laughter. And as I watch her put her hand on his chest, giving him a delicate little push, I imagine her saying, "Omigod, Cash, stop! You're making me *so* ditzy! Oops! I meant dizzy!"

But Rey, totally oblivious to the three-act play that's been unfolding at Table A for the last ten minutes, and seemingly determined to get to the bottom of all this "Gobsmacked," daddy-rock-star business, goes, "I wonder why your mom never mentioned that before?" Then he looks at me, waiting for an answer.

So I drag my gaze away from Sloane, and turn to face him, determined to give him my full attention for a change. "That's because my mom hates pop," I tell him, looking into his deep dark eyes. "And she hates *my* pop even more."

Wednesday, September Whatever, 2006

3:47 P.M.

Current Mood—Elated

Current Music—"Hero Takes a Fall" by the Bangles (so appropriate)

Quote of the Day: "Three may keep a secret, if two of them are dead."

—Benjamin Franklin

Come as You Are

Okay, so as not to bore you with a long-ass list of boring details, I'll just give you the gist and move on: My former best friend (who will from this point forward be referred to as Princess Pink, or P. P. if I'm lazy), has catapulted into the social stratosphere, earning herself a spot so coveted, so sanctified, and so exalted, while leaving yours truly both literally, and metaphorically, in the dust.

Now, just in case you're ready to click off, thinking this blog will amount to nothing more than some big, fat, pathetic, crybaby crap about how I was cast out and betrayed—well, think again. 'Cause if you'll just bear with me, and read a little further, you'll see that it actually aims much deeper than that.

This is a story of humble beginnings, a quick, yet well-choreographed ascent, and (if I'm lucky), the inevitable fall.

This is how it began:

Eight years ago I sat in my living room, spying on the house across the street as a tired-looking mom and her tiny daughter climbed out of an old, beat-up U-Haul and carried their meager belongings inside.

Cut to the next day at school, when that same girl is looking so scared and lonely that I invite her over to my table, so that she can sit with my friends and me during lunch. That's right, I had other friends. Kids were nicer back then, less mean and judgmental. But let us not forget the main point, that I'm the one who rescued *her*.

But it's not like she'll ever admit to that. In fact, now that she's so cool and popular and important she won't admit to much of anything.

And that's where I come in. As a sort of recorder of history, a spiller of secrets, the one and only person with access to the long list of P. P.'s misdeeds, as well as the burning desire to set the record straight.

So, without further ado, I present to you a random list of secrets, in no particular order of importance or occurrence, that Princess Pink most definitely does *not* want you to know, a.k.a. The List:

1. That's not her real hair color.
2. That's not her real eye color.
3. Her first kiss was with her first cousin when she was in sixth grade, and he was in seventh. They were inside her closet, crushed against her hanging sweater shelf, and yes, they used their tongues.

More from me soon,

Eleanor Rigby

Twelve

The second I clicked Post I felt exhilarated. I mean, to think that I'd actually put something out there that others just might possibly want to read was so unbelievably exciting that I felt all revved-up and giddy inside. And I got so addicted to the idea of some stranger reading it that I kept checking it myself, rereading it again and again as though I wasn't really the author, and that I didn't actually know either me or Princess Pink. Like I was learning this story for the very first time. And I gotta admit, I got so carried away that for a brief moment, I actually considered sending it to Rey. You know, just so he could read through it and give me his expert blogger opinion.

But then I thought better of it. I mean, if I wanted to stay anonymous, then I couldn't confide in anyone, not even Rey. Because staying anonymous meant staying honest. And really, wasn't that the whole point?

"So how often do you talk to your dad?" Rey asks, breaking apart a cranberry-orange scone and handing me half.

We're on our way to school, carrying our coffees and sharing breakfast, just like Sloane and I used to. "We go through phases." I shrug. "It's like sometimes we talk a lot, couple times a week, and then later it will just sort of die down and a couple months might pass without so much as a single e-mail. Why?" I ask, gazing into his brown eyes and wondering why he's suddenly so interested in my parental situation.

"No reason." He shrugs. "I just think it's kind of cool that he was in a band and all. And also I guess because now that I know your mom pretty well I'm kind of curious about your dad. Do you guys get along?"

"Yeah, he's pretty cool." And then, realizing that once again, we're talking about me, I look up at him and go, "Well, what about you? What're your parents like?"

"Well, my dad's a psychiatrist, author, and sometime professor, and my mom's an artist and screenwriter," he says, taking a sip of his coffee, and popping a piece of scone in his mouth.

I just stare at him, totally amazed. I mean, I'm starting to think that either this guy is a major pathological liar, or he truly is one of the coolest, most interesting people I've ever met. "You're mom's a screenwriter?" I ask, still gazing at him, still amazed.

But he just nods and gives me the last remaining piece of his scone since I've already gobbled all of mine.

"Like anything I've ever heard of or seen before?" I ask, wiping the crumbs from my mouth.

He just shrugs. "Probably," he says, as humble as ever.

And just as I'm about to ask him for names, titles, locations, and all kinds of important insider details, Cash Davis's shiny black Hummer pulls into the school parking lot, and splashes gutter water all over us.

But believe me, that's not even the worst of it. Because when he finally parks that big stupid beast and the passenger door flings open, I gawk in amazement when I see that the person who jumps out is Sloane.

And I just stand there staring as she performs her much practiced and now completely overdone hair toss, then reaches inside, kicking up one flirtatious foot as she retrieves her books, and breaks into delighted, phony giggles when Cash comes around the side, reaches out his hand, and grabs her right smack on the ass.

And as I watch all of this unfold, all I can think is:

If Rey is right—and Sloane is hooking up with Cash— then Jaci, Holly, and Claire are destined to turn on her.

And believe me, I plan to be front row center when it happens.

But Rey just shakes his head, brushes the gutter water off his tie, and goes, "Come on, show's over." Then he tugs on my arm and pulls me away, like a dog from a weird smell.

"So, I'm thinking I'll come by around ten," Rey says, taking a sip of his water and gazing at me.

"What?" I ask, eyes glued to Sloane and Cash, thinking how ironic it is that I'm now using Table C to spy on her, when originally it was *us* spying on *them.*

"The band? The one I told you about? Are you even listening to me?" he asks, obviously annoyed.

"Of course I'm listening," I say, patting his hand distractedly while tearing a piece off my sandwich. Watching Sloane wrap her arms around her tiny waist and bend forward, as she fake-laughs at something Cash just said, using the moment to discreetly tug on the hem of her top, pulling it down just barely an inch, so that she can reveal a tad more cleavage.

"You know what, just forget it," Rey says, shaking his head and looking away, clearly over me now.

And by the time I tear my eyes away from Sloane and focus on him, I realize I may have gone just a bit too far with my whole Table A fixation. I mean, I know how on the surface it probably seems like I'm obsessed with her, just because I watch her a lot and then report on everything she does. And how in the course of just a few days of knowing each other, Rey's been forced to suffer through the retelling of our entire friendship history so many times he can probably recite it in his sleep. And even though he's been extremely patient, and has even participated by offering more of his amazing insight, I guess by now, he's pretty much reached his limit. And if I don't get a grip, rein it in, and start paying a little more attention to him, I'll risk losing my one and only friend on the planet.

And the truth is, he really is my only friend. And I'm completely amazed at how in such a short amount of time he's almost managed to replace Sloane. And the only reason I even say "almost" is because he's a guy, so naturally there are certain things we just don't talk about. But even though he has my mom's seal of approval (which I fully admit, really does kind of bug me), we actually have so much in common, so many shared interests that it's almost kind of eerie. I mean, we both love eighties music (but only the good stuff like the Jam and the Clash, and *not* Toto). We both read a ton of books, both fiction and nonfiction. We both prefer the kind of small, interesting movies that *don't* star Tom Cruise, Vin Diesel, or pull in big summer crowds. And we both write our own blogs (although he still doesn't know about mine).

But even after all that, one of the best things about Rey is how he's so comfortable just being himself, wearing his black suits to school and lugging around his guitar, and how he truly doesn't care what other people think. I mean, Sloane and I pretty much cared about what everyone thought, and even though it may have worked for her, it pretty much failed for me. And even though I freely admit that I really do still care about everyone else's opinion, it's pretty cool and inspiring to hang out with someone who doesn't.

But I don't share any of that with him. I mean, I just can't. So instead I look him right in the eye and say. "Got it. Ten o'clock. I'll even meet you at the café so you don't have to come by my house or anything."

Then I hold his gaze for as long as I can, before turning back toward Sloane.

THE GOSPEL OF ELEANOR RIGBY

Friday, September Something, 2006
3:58 P.M.
Current Mood—Snarky
Current Music—Some song by the English Beat
Quote of the Day—"You can observe a lot by watching."—Yogi Berra

Wake Me Up When September Ends

105

It's official, Princess Pink is now dating Captain World. That is, if
ass-grabbing, fake-laughing, hair-tossing, lunch-table straddling,
SUV-riding, and cleavage-flaunting are in any way indicative of a relationship in progress.

Also, for today, the final count for number of times P. P. passed
right by and pretended not to see me? 4.

But the number of times I caught her gazing at my friend and me
with intense curiosity when she thought I wasn't looking? 2.

And since I'm burdened with a ton of homework, not to mention
the very rare occurrence of after-plans, I'll just cut to the chase and
present to you the next installment of The List:

4. That cleavage P. P. is flaunting? So not hers. Mad props can
   be sent to:
   > Victoria's Secret
   > Miracle Water Bra section
   > Fashion Island
   > Newport Beach, California
5. In seventh grade, P. P. had such a major crush on the principal
   she sent him a secret Valentine gift of a little, furry stuffed
   bear. His black eyes were shiny, his stitched-on mouth was
   smiling, and his arms were stretched wide-open, bearing a

banner that read, "I wuv you this much!" But when the principal discovered who sent it, he wasted no time in ordering an emergency conference that included P. P.'s mom, the vice-principal, a random female staff member, and Princess Pink herself, who was forced to apologize for "sending a very inappropriate Valentine's Day gift that bore a very inappropriate message," before signing on the dotted line, solemnly swearing that "the only physical contact that ever occurred between them happened only in her head."

Enjoy your day,

Eleanor Rigby

Thirteen

I head for the café early, hoping that I can maybe use some family connections to get poor Rey out of there a few minutes before his shift ends, only to walk in and find him, my mom, and Autumn sitting at one of the empty tables, sipping Let It Be green tea and laughing at one of my mom's lame stories.

"Hey." I smile, wondering if Rey truly thinks she's all that funny, or if he's just hoping to win Employee of the Month. "Um, are you ready to go?" I ask, my eyes darting between my mom and him.

My mom slowly gets up from the table in a way that favors her occasional bad back, and that never fails to make me feel guilty for not being nicer. "Go ahead, you guys have fun," she says, as she and Autumn gather the empty cups and head behind the counter, while Rey goes into the bathroom to change.

I head for the back room and wait by the door, so we can bail out of there like the second he's done. And when he finally emerges in a crisp black T-shirt, a pair of dark-rinse jeans, and some Van's tennis shoes with skulls all over them, I just sort of stand there and stare, feeling all speechless and weird. Partly because it seems odd that he gets all dressed up in a suit and tie for school, then goes casual on the weekend, but also because it kind of feels like I'm just now seeing him for the very first time. But I guess that's probably only because that day when I really did see him for the very first time I was so upset and freaked-out about Sloane and Cash that I could barely even focus. And then later in class, he was just this kind of annoying lab partner I thought I was stuck with. And then after that he somehow turned into my friend. So I guess I never really looked at him until now.

But still, I think it's pretty obvious that I'm just now noticing how hot he is because I was way too distracted to notice before. So clearly this is really no more than just a simple, delayed reaction. And could never be considered, in any way whatsoever, as indicative of anything more.

Yet even knowing all that, it's still sort of weird how now that he's standing before me, dressed so nice, smelling so good, and gazing at me and smiling, I'm getting this kind of weird sensation in the pit of my stomach, and I'm not exactly sure what it means. All I know is that it wasn't there before and now it is.

He reaches for the door, holds it open, and goes, "After you."

And I practically run outside, totally relieved to be in the alley, where the sky is just dark enough to hide my face.

"So where is this place?" I ask, feeling ridiculously nervous to be walking alone with him, and even more foolish when I find myself wondering if this is a date.

"Couple blocks up." He nods. And when he sees skinny smoker dude standing in his usual spot, right outside the back door of the liquor store, he waves and goes, "Hey, almost done?"

But dude just crushes his cigarette between the ground and his big, sturdy boot, shakes his head, and says, "I'm never done." Then he glances briefly at me before heading back inside.

"You know that guy?" I whisper, squinting at Rey, wondering why on earth he'd even be talking to him.

But Rey just shrugs. "Doesn't everyone?"

Then he throws his arm around my shoulder and leads me across the street, as that weird feeling in the pit of my stomach just grows even stronger.

By the time we're standing outside the Dirty Bird, I'm thinking there's no way they're letting us in. I mean, this is like a *real* club, the kind where they serve alcohol and check your driver's license at the door. And since the only license in my wallet was issued from the uniformed attendant working the Autotopia ride at Disneyland, you can see why I might hesitate.

But Rey just walks right up to the bouncer and shakes his hand, and before I can even blink we're inside.

And it's not until we're well past the door that I whisper, "How did you do that?"

But Rey just laughs. "As long as you don't try to order a drink, it's all good," he says.

And remembering my last humiliating foray into alcoholism, I know that won't be a problem tonight.

I follow him into the main room where we settle into a cracked leather booth, and then I gaze all around, thinking how weird it is that I've passed by this place like a bazillion times before, but never once thought about going inside. But now that I was actually in, I was feeling so cool and grown-up to be here. And it's not like it's really all that great or anything, because the truth is, it's not. I mean, the floor is kind of covered in this old, cracked tile, and the tables all seem like they probably have a thick layer of gum stuck underneath (and I say *probably* because it's not like I'm gonna climb under and check), and the leather on these seats is kind of old and shabby and ripped in places. But the thing that makes it so exciting and cool is that I never would have come here if I were still hanging out with Sloane, since the only music she ever listens to are songs by former Mickey Mouse Club members. Not to mention how she never wants to go anywhere that hasn't been declared "hot" by Paris Hilton, *InStyle* magazine, or the cast of *The Real O. C.*

So I look at Rey, and go, "This place is so awesome, everyone looks so laid-back and cool. I mean, you'd never see Sloane and Jaci and those guys in a place like this." I shake my head and gaze around, taking it all in. "You know, because even though it's obvious how they all *think* they're cool, they're definitely not this kind of cool. They're like boring, mainstream, mass-marketed, fake cool." Then I nod and smile and wait for him to agree.

Only he doesn't agree. He just shakes his head, rubs his eyes, and glances at his watch for like the millionth time in the last five minutes.

And the second I see that, I know I've gone too far. I mean, all I have to do is look at his face to know that he's totally exasperated and completely over the whole Table A thing. So in a lame attempt to lighten the mood and get a jokier feel going, I point at his watch and go, "So, what's with the clock-watching? Waiting for someone?" And then I laugh, since obviously, he's not. I mean, it's just us.

But then he looks right at me and says, "Well, actually, Shay said she'd get here early and save us a seat, but I don't see her. I hope she's not getting hassled at the door." Then he squints in that direction, like he's about to get up and go check or something.

I stare at him, feeling more than a little shaky. "Um, who's Shay?" I ask, in a small, quiet voice.

He looks up and points. "That's Shay."

I follow the length of his finger, and at the very tip I find this extremely cool, very beautiful girl.

"Hey," she says, sliding in next to Rey and kissing him on the cheek in a way that's not exactly intimate but still makes me wonder just who the heck she is.

I mean, obviously, Rey and I are nothing more than just completely platonic, casual friends. And if he wants to have a beautiful, hip, edgy girlfriend who likes to kiss him on the cheek, then that's totally fine with me. Because, it's not like I care or anything. All I'm saying is that it would have been nice to be clued into this situation a little earlier. Just as a courtesy, that's all.

So Rey introduces us and I nod and smile, even though I'm totally scrutinizing her dyed black, china doll haircut, smudgy, smoky eye makeup, perfectly lined red lips, and pale, pale skin. And even though most girls who frequent this zip code spend a ton of time and money striving for "tan, beachy, and natural," believe me, on her, the opposite look totally works.

"Shay goes to Sage Hill," Rey says, glancing from her to me.

Oh, so she's rich, I think. *Well, rich or on scholarship.*

"She lives in Pelican Hill."

Bingo, rich.

I try to smile benignly, even though I'm inspecting her like the key piece of evidence in a particularly gruesome crime scene. "How do you guys know each other?" I ask, watching as she and Rey glance at each other and laugh.

"Shay's dad optioned one of my mom's screenplays," he says. "But that's just a coincidence. Because we actually met when she came into the café and ordered a smoothie."

"Purple Berry Haze." She smiles, exposing the slight distance between her two front teeth, which, so far, is the only flaw I've been able to detect on her otherwise perfect face. But still, wouldn't you know it, on her it looks cool. "I just love the name." She laughs.

Knowing my mom's stupid organic café (and cloying, cutesy dessert names), are responsible for Shay's being here now just makes me even more miserable. But I know I have to say something, I mean, after all, she's a smoothie fan. So I just nod and go, "Yup, that's one of our top sellers."

And then I stare at the stage until the band comes on.

The second the band takes a break, I beeline for the bathroom. And then the second I'm inside, I notice that Shay is right behind me.

"You go first," she says, ushering me into the tiny, narrow stall. So I do. And then just as I get in position and start going about my business, she says, "So what's up with you and Rey?"

Okay, first of all, I really hate it when people want to small talk while you pee. It's just so freaking awkward, full of all kinds of pauses and weird moments. And second, a serious question like that requires eye contact, because I really need to see her face so that I can know just exactly what it is she's trying to get at. But now that she's asked, I feel like I have to answer. I mean, I can't just ignore it, can I? So I sigh and go, "Well, um . . ." And then I try to drag out that "um" for as long as I can, without sounding like I'm meditating.

Then when I finally come out I continue by saying, "Well, we're really good friends." And then I head for the sink, thinking she's gonna go inside the stall and leave me in peace. But she doesn't. She just leans against the wall and stares at me.

"*And . . .* " she says, waiting for more.

"*And* what?" I ask, grabbing a handful of paper towels to dry my hands with.

"*And* that's it? Just friends?" She looks me over like she doesn't quite believe me.

And even though I guess in a way that's actually kind of flattering, I mean, for someone like *her* to think that a guy (any guy) might actually covet *me,* I'm starting to feel a little weird about all this. Because now that she's asking, I remember how I felt back at the café, when he came out of the bathroom, looking and smelling so good, and how my stomach went all weird again when I watched her kiss him on the cheek. And it makes me wonder if we really are just friends.

Or if part of me actually wants to be something else, something more.

"Because he talks about you a lot, and . . ."

"Yeah?" I say, desperate to hear the rest of this, hoping it will help me decipher my true feelings.

But she just shrugs, leaving the sentence unfinished, suspended.

So I just reach into my purse, grabbing the lip gloss Sloane gave me but that I still use. (I mean, why waste perfectly good lip gloss?), and coat my lips with a thick, gloppy line of peach shine.

Then Shay looks at me and goes, "Okay, so if you're just friends, then I guess you won't mind if I ask him out? 'Cause I really, really like him. He's just so adorable, and smart, and talented. Sexy, too." She giggles.

So I giggle, too. But only because I know I'm supposed to. Because believe me, inside my body my stomach's gone all queasy, while my mind is spinning with thoughts like, *Do I mind?* And, *Would I even be able to admit it if I did?* I mean, I never really thought about any of this until she just now forced it on me. And even though I'm kind of leaning toward the fact that, yes, I might, actually, really kind of mind, for some reason, I just can't bring myself to tell her that. Because I just can't be sure if I really, truly like him, or if I just now decided I do since recently discovering that not only is he in high demand, but apparently, he's also mine to give or keep at the drop of a word.

So I compromise, by giving her the wordless shrug. Which, to my understanding, has always been the universal sign for taking the fifth.

But apparently Shay doesn't quite interpret it that way. Because she just smiles and says, "Omigod, thanks!"

And by the time we get back to our booth, she slides in extra close to Rey. I mean, she's practically sitting in his lap now. But it's not like I'm watching or anything. I just keep my eyes glued to the band for the rest of their set.

THE GOSPEL OF ELEANOR RIGBY

Weekend of September ??, 2006
12:04 P.M.
Current Mood—Don't ask
Current Music—Sex Pistols singing "Anarchy in the UK" so loud my
earplugs are vibrating.
Quote of the Day—"There is no little enemy."—Benjamin Franklin

Complicated

115

Um, did I give the impression that this blog would be wholly dedicated to the story of Princess Pink and the ultimate rise and fall of a
teenage drama queen? Because if so, I'm here to tell you that I may
have to revise that just a little. I may actually be forced to write myself just a little more prominently into my own story. Just like that
guy in *Adaptation* did with his movie.

Not to mention how, since I don't exactly hang with Princess Pink
anymore, the weekend edition could run a little dry from time to
time. But that's where I come in. Literally.

So, to bring you up-to-speed, last night I auctioned off the one
guy in the universe who may very well have turned out to be—the potential love of my life.

Though, now that I think about it, *auction* isn't really the right
word. Since technically, I walked away from that little transaction
with even less than I started—with no more to show for it than a bad
mood, an aching heart, and what appears to be a permanent pang in
the pit of my stomach. So I guess I should rephrase that, as obviously it wasn't really an "auction" at all. In fact, it wasn't even a gift
with purchase. It was more like one of those gift bags, like the kind
you get for attending a really cool party, or for being an Oscar pre-
senter at the Academy Awards.

Only it wasn't cool.

And it hardly felt like the Oscars.

But the real highlight came when this one particular song came on, that for reasons I cannot disclose (privacy and anonymity issues), induced me to glance at Gift Bag, only to find him involved in a serious game of tonsil hockey with *her*.

And not long after that, I fled.

And The List goes on:

6. For those of you who can still remember that awful day in junior high when the entire school bus was throbbing with the smell of dog crap so bad the driver was forced to open all the windows so we could hang our heads out and gag? Well, my friends, the real culprit behind that dreadful, smelly stank was the smashed-up piece of freshly baked dog turd that was stuck to the sole of Princess Pink's silver Converse tennis shoe.

7. When: Ash Wednesday, seventh grade

   Who: P. P.

   What: Pretending to be a devout Catholic, P. P. came to school bearing a rather large ash smudge on her forehead. Only thing is, P. P. is Protestant. Which means she was using *Jesus* to cover a zit.

8. During the eighth-grade presidential fitness test, right in the middle of performing consecutive elbow to raised knee sit-ups, when the quiet sound of physical exertion and stomach crunch counting was pierced by an unexpected, rather sudden, embarrassingly loud, and smelly fart? You guessed it, that was the work of P. P. and her penchant for breakfast burritos.

Best wishes,

Eleanor Rigby

Fourteen

Monday morning when I stopped by Dietrich's I wasn't sure just what to expect. I mean, first of all, I couldn't be sure if Rey would even be there. And second, I had no idea how he'd act toward me if he was. Not to mention how I might inadvertently act around him.

I mean, I'd just spent the entire weekend poring over his blog, looking for clues as to how he might feel about me (um, there were no clues), and dissecting my conversation with Shay, going over it again and again, and each time coming to the same lame conclusion—that I'd accidentally, unintentionally, yet wholeheartedly, given my sincere permission, and signed-on-the-dotted-line consent, for Shay and Rey to hook up and make out directly in front of me.

Only now I want to take it all back.

And *not* because I want to be the one making out with him or anything remotely like that. I mean, I'm pretty much existing in a state of emotional limbo, still feeling completely undecided on all that. But the one thing I do know for sure is that I want Rey to sit back and wait, abstaining from all romantic and physical female contact, while I take my time deciding.

"Hey," he says, waving at me from our usual table, like everything's totally normal. "I already got our coffee and scone." He smiles.

Our *coffee and scone? I wonder how Shay would feel about that?*

I slide onto the opposite stool as he pushes my latte toward me. And I gaze at him from over the top of my cup, noticing how happy he looks today. Maybe even too happy.

"So," he says, breaking off a piece of frosted maple oat scone, and leaving the rest for me. "You left early. You missed out."

Missed out on what? I think. *Overtime in tonsil hockey?*

"Your friends got busted."

My eyes bug out, as I drop the scone and stare.

"Well, they got container checked. They were all lined up on Main Beach. We saw them when we were leaving. I guess the cops stopped them for questioning, and then decided to check their water bottles for a suspicious substance."

"Serious?" I ask, hoping the story will get even worse than this, and somehow involve handcuffs, billy clubs, a permanent stain on their permanent records, maybe even an extended stay in juvenile hall.

"Yeah, but apparently it was nothing since they just ended up emptying all the bottles and letting them go."

"But who was all there?" I ask, desperate for every single detail, but only because of the blog. I mean, other than that it's not like I really care or anything.

But Rey just shrugs. "Who knows? They all look alike to me. I can't tell the difference."

And as we walk out the door and head for school, I'm wondering if this is maybe something Eleanor Rigby should write about. I mean, since she wasn't actually there to witness it I'm not sure if that goes against like, the laws of journalistic integrity or something.

But when we arrive on campus, I see Sloane surrounded by students. And I watch from a distance as she stands before them, her glistening blond hair reflecting the sun, as she recants the whole sordid tale for a scandal-hungry crowd. And even though I can't exactly hear what it is she's saying, I can tell by the look on her face that she's using only top-shelf adjectives and adverbs to embellish her starring role in her fictionalized version of "Busted on the Beach! A Cheerleader's Story."

And as I vacate the scene, I've already decided not to write about it. I mean, somehow that whole mess has just made her even more popular, and I'll be damned if I'll do anything to help that along.

Wednesday, finally October, 2006
4:15 P.M.
Current Mood—Mostly unhappy
Current Music—None
Quote of the Day—"I love treason, but hate a traitor."
                                        —Julius Caesar

You Oughta Know

Okay, so apparently, not only is Princess Pink too good for me, but she's also too good to acknowledge me. I was in the bathroom at the beginning of lunch when I vacated the stall only to find her practically canoodling with her own reflection as she leaned in really close to the mirror and painted on a shiny, thick, sticky layer of DuWop Lip Venom (that she probably stole), while pretending she didn't see me, even though it's pretty obvious that she did.

Me: "So." Okay, try not to judge me. I mean, I felt like I had to say something and this was the best I could do on such short notice.

P. P.: "____." She says nothing. Just sighs, and removes a stray eyelash from her dermatologist-tended cheek.

Me: "That's it? You can't even say hello anymore?" Followed by penetrating, malevolent glare.

P. P.: Still not breaking from her mirror-gazing love fest. "Jeez, Eleanor, what do you want from me?" This was followed by a classic headshake-deep sigh combo (at her own reflection, yet meant for me). Like she's Paris Hilton and I'm some jilted Greek shipping heir who won't leave her alone.

Well, P. P. since you asked, here's My List:
I Want

1. An apology for your sudden defection after eight years of friendship with no explanation or final note.
2. My Black Eyed Peas CD, which you've had since the beginning of last summer and have yet to return.
3. A simple thank-you for the countless hours I spent tutoring you so that you wouldn't face the humiliation of flunking out of English for Dummies.
4. A little acknowledgment for when I put everything on hold so that I could help you through a really rough time when you discovered that your real dad is not out of the country like your mom said, but that he's actually locked up in some Nevada Federal Prison for Men where he's serving time for tax fraud and evasion.
5. Author credit for the cheer you stole, plagiarized, and used without my consent.
6. A smidgen of gratitude for helping you through yet another rough time when you discovered that your mom was having an affair with a married man (and father of two), who also happened to be her boss, and who she eventually got knocked up by and married (in that order).
7. An ounce of appreciation for doing my best to make you feel better when I tried to convince you that your mom's not-so-secret past as an exotic dancer meant that she'd probably performed in the chorus in some way off-Broadway productions.
8. A simple hello, wave of acknowledgement, or halfhearted nod when we pass in the hall so I don't have to feel like the last eight years I spent being your best friend was a total waste of my time.

Faithfully yours,

Eleanor Rigby

Fifteen

So, every day at lunch for the past week and a half, I just sit at our table, hunching over my healthy, heart-smart sandwich and accompanying bag of contraband chips that I shove in there when my mom's not looking, and eavesdrop on Rey's excruciatingly cute, increasingly romantic, seemingly never-ending, cell phone conversations with Shay.

And the worst part is, since I'm the one who accidentally blessed this whole unholy union to begin with, I'm pretty much forced to just sit back and act like I couldn't care less and can't possibly be bothered to notice that the calls just get longer and longer as the two of them just grow closer and closer with each and every passing day.

I mean, since clearly this is all my fault to begin with, what choice do I have but to nod and smile and basically just play along every time he snaps his phone shut and relays all manner of adorable facts, useless information, and vital statistics that I never, *ever* wanted to know? Like:

"Did you know that Shay's new golden retriever puppy is named Nola, after the Scarlett Johansson character in *Match Point*?

"Did you know that Shay's spending the summer volunteering in New Orleans? Aiding flood victims and helping to rebuild the city?

"Did you know that Shay modeled in Paris two years ago? And that she had so many jobs she could barely keep it straight, when she decided to give it all up so that she could have a normal high-school experience and graduate with her class like everyone else?

"Did you know that Shay is perfect in every single freaking way, and that she's the bestest thing that ever happened to me in this whole wide world?"

Okay, maybe he didn't exactly say that last one, but still, he may as well have.

And after last night's tortured reading of his latest blog entry that veered from his usual insightful, relevant, highly entertaining subject matter, to a full page musing on the challenges of house-training Shay's adorable puppy, Nola, I knew I just wasn't up for any more of that. So I grabbed my lunch, and hauled it over to the library where I could eat in peace. And even though, technically, you're not supposed to do that, the librarians don't seem to mind when it's me. But that's probably because I'm one of the few people in this entire school who actually knows them by name.

And then just a few minutes before the bell rings, I'm gathering up my trash when I hear someone whispering from somewhere among the bookshelves. And even though normally I wouldn't pay any attention to that since it's a library, and that's what people are pretty much forced to do in libraries, there's something about the way this sounds, something kind of frantic, upset, and whimpery that makes me want to investigate further.

I grab my stuff, fling my backpack over my shoulder, and

figure I'll just stop by for a quick peek on my way out the door. And just as I round the corner and peer down the aisle, I see some girl all curled up on the floor, crying into the sleeve of her sweater, and pressing her cell phone tight to her ear. And I stand there in shock when I realize it's Sloane.

Then she says, "Okay. I will. Bye, Dad." Then she closes her phone, buries her face in her hands, and breaks into these major, shoulder-shaking tears.

And acting on nothing but pure instinct and an obviously impaired memory, I head right for her, kneel down beside her, and in a tentative voice go, "Sloane?"

And when she looks up, I see that her eyes are all puffy and red.

"Are you okay?" I ask, gazing at her and knowing she's not.

But she just shakes her head, and hides her face in her hands again, breaking into even louder, more violent sobs.

And even though I feel kind of awkward and uncomfortable to even be here in the first place, that doesn't stop me from asking, "Do you need to talk?" Then I sit there patiently waiting for her to respond. I mean, I know it seems crazy that after everything that's happened I would even care enough to ask, but I guess there's still this small part of me that retains a little hope. Besides, I think it's safe to assume that this is not the kind of stuff she can share with her cool, new friends. 'Cause from what I've seen they're pretty strict about limiting all of their conversations to the topics of tanning, shopping, food purging, and guys.

But even so, I can still hardly believe it, when she actually looks up and smiles, before wiping her eyes with the sleeve of her sweater, which transfers most of her mascara to her thick, ribbed cuff.

And when the bell finally rings, she looks at me and whispers, "You're the only one who knows."

Then she gathers her things and heads for the door saying, "I'll call you tonight."

Wednesday, October??, 2006
10:05 P.M.
Current Mood—Gobsmacked
Current Music—My sister's lame iPod mix
Quote of the Day—"You cannot teach a crab to walk straight."
                                        —Aristophanes

Oops! . . . I Did It Again

Seen: curled up and crying, our recently crowned Princess Pink on the verge of a complete emotional collapse, and ready to lean on old Eleanor's shoulder.

Did she, you wonder?

Not a chance.

And in honor of ex-best friends who dingdong ditch you, I present to you a special edition of The List, with one extra bonus secret thrown in for free.

9. As part of her self-created popularity boot camp, P. P. spent the entire summer memorizing a homemade stack of 3×5 note cards with imaginary questions written on the front, and their appropriate responses scrawled on the back. Think of it like flash cards for social retards. For example, the front of a card might read, "Omigod, love your skirt!" And when you flip it over to the back you'll note that the correct response is, "Oh, please, this is so old!"

10. P. P., who is taking prealgebra *again* this year, somehow managed to craft an intricate, detailed, color-coded graph depicting every teen movie queen going back to the mid-

eighties, noting not only their commonalities, but also their individual strengths and weaknesses, which she then translated into a *USA Today*-type brightly colored pie chart showing the ratio of blonde to brunette, cheerleader to class president, athlete to mathlete, so that she'd know just exactly who to emulate.

11. If asked, P. P. will pretend that she never, ever, not even once, cried herself to sleep because the only thing she wanted in the whole wide world was to meet Britney Spears. But don't you believe her.

12. In second grade, Princess Pink's show-and-tell presentation was cut short when she stood before the classroom with her mom's fully charged vibrator in hand, offering a free neck, back, and shoulder massage for anyone interested.

Good night and good luck!

Your friend,

Eleanor Rigby

Sixteen

The next day, I admit, I'm totally scanning the campus for Sloane. But even though I don't actually see her anywhere, it's not until lunch that I can truly confirm that she's a no-show. I mean, she isn't in the library, and I happen to know that because, like the total retard I am, I checked. And she also isn't anywhere near her lunch table, which makes me wonder if she's home sick, or maybe even somewhere in the desert, scaling the barbed-wire fence surrounding her dad's new government-sponsored home.

Basically I guess I'm just wondering why she never called.

But then I'm also wondering why I even care.

And I'm so preoccupied with all of this self-created drama in my head, that it isn't until I actually sit at my table that I notice the new addition.

"Hey," I say, gazing at this guy with shaggy, dark hair that partially obscures his face, smooth olive skin (save for the two zits on his chin), nice, kind-looking, hazel eyes, and a black

T-shirt with a picture of the leader of that eighties band, A Flock of Seagulls, which I really hope is meant to be ironic.

"Winter, Elijah," Rey says, taking a bite of his sandwich and nodding toward the newcomer.

And no sooner do I say "Hey" again, when we're joined by two more guys, both brown-haired, one skinny, one normal, and a girl with long, black, straight hair, heavily lined dark eyes, and pale, pale lips. And then Rey informs me that their names are Clark, Evan, and Hayden, respectively, and I'm wondering if we've just formed a new band.

As soon as they settle in they all start talking about music, universally agreeing that Hendrix is a god and that every single one of the American Idols is a sucky sellout. And I just sit there, eating my lunch and not saying a word. I mean, it's not that I hate Jimi Hendrix, it's just that my mom *loves* him, which makes it kind of hard for me to even sort of like him. But then, when they move on to books and movies and TV shows, I start feeling so good about hanging with a new group of people who I actually have things in common with, that it's not until after the bell rings and I'm on my way to class that I realize how I totally forgot to stare at Table A. I mean, seriously, that whole entire time, I didn't so much as glance over there, not even once. Though I guess that could actually have more to do with Sloane's absence than any newfound camaraderie.

After school, I'm walking home with Rey, who's actually headed straight for the café to start his shift, and Evan, who, I just discovered, lives right around the block from me, when my cell phone rings.

And the way they both turn and look at me, complete surprise so clearly defined on their faces (especially Rey's), makes me feel so embarrassed that I'm no longer sure if I'll answer it. I mean, as pathetic as this is to admit, I think it's safe to assume that it's probably just my mom or Autumn. So why should I risk flipping it open and saying "hello" just so I can confirm all of our suspicions that: (*a*) it's definitely one of my three closest blood relatives, and (*b*) I truly am the world's most unpopular, undesirable, grade-A geek.

But then right before it's about to go into voice mail, I realize how I just might be overthinking this. So I flip it open and go, "Yeah?" in this kind of breathless, hurried way.

Then this male voice, that I don't even recognize, goes, "Hey, it's me. Easton."

So I glance at Rey and Evan, switch the phone to my other ear, and sort of turn away from them, in an attempt to look a little more mysterious as well as get some privacy.

"Hey," I say. I mean, that's pretty much all I can come up with since it's not like I thought I'd ever hear from him again.

And he goes, "Guess where I am."

And since I'm supposed to guess, I go, "Um, New Delhi?"

And he laughs and says, "No, L.A. I'm up here for an audition, and a friend of mine loaned me a car so I thought I'd head down and see you."

And I go, "Seriously?" And then I glance at my friends again since we planned to all hang out at Rey's tonight and I'm starting to realize how this could actually work out to be so amazingly perfect in so many ways.

"Seriously, I arrived yesterday, but I'm leaving the day after tomorrow. I know it's short notice and all, so if you can't make it work, it's cool."

I peek at Rey and Evan, who are talking about how Chris Martin lost his already tenuous hold on rocker credibility the day he married Gwyneth, but then I catch Rey sneaking a peek at me, so I turn away again and go, "Um, no, actually it's perfect. But I told some friends I'd hang with them tonight, if that's okay?"

And he goes, "Just give me your address. I'll MapQuest it and see you by nine."

And when I close the phone, I can't help but smile. Especially after seeing Rey's expression.

"You should wear the Republican jeans, the wedge heels, and that white tunic top," Autumn says, lounging on her bed and looking at me.

"He's seen those jeans like a million times already. And, by the way, the Republican joke is totally played." I shake my head and glare at my closet and my pathetic collection of useless, go-with-nothing, outdated clothes. "God, I hate my stuff," I say, kicking at a line of shoes, watching as they tumble, one after the other, like gymnasts performing a well-practiced floor routine.

"Believe me, guys don't even notice stuff like that," Autumn says, nodding her head with authority, like she just might really know a thing or two about this.

But I just roll my eyes and turn back toward my closet, not hating it any less than I did a second ago.

"Seriously, they just don't care nearly as much as you think," she insists.

And when I turn to look at her again, I wonder if she's right. I mean, after all, this is the same little artsy freak, who somehow, against all reason, logic, and odds, spurred the undying affection of Cash Davis's little hottie brother, Crosby. And to hear her tell it, the drama is anything but over.

"Okay," she says, standing up and taking charge, since obviously someone has to. "This is what you do. You wear the dark denim stovepipes, the black, spiky, ankle boots. And the white ribbed tank with the black bra, and make sure the strap is showing. Then add all three of your chunky silver chain necklaces, which means no earrings 'cause you don't want to overload the whole face-to-neck ratio, but definitely throw in some cool bangles to kind of load up your arms. And then top the whole thing off with either a funky cardigan, that shrunken, black, tight little blazer, or your old denim jacket, in case you get cold. And oh, yeah, flat iron your hair, and wear one of those hats like Madonna does when she's out riding her bike in the English countryside." She looks at me, nodding with the confidence of prepubescent authority.

While I stand there, trying to piece it all together. "Who am I supposed to be?" I finally ask. "Chrissie Hynde?"

But Autumn just shakes her head, plops down on her bed, and focuses back on her book. "Just trust me," she says.

So I did. I trusted her. And believe me, it worked. Because right after Easton met my mom (which by the way, was not at all the nightmare I'd anticipated), we were headed for the borrowed car (which turned out to be some big, silver, four-door BMW sedan that belongs to his agent), he leaned in, smiled, and said, "You look hot."

And then he kissed me on the cheek, and held the door open as I got situated in the passenger seat.

And even though I felt all giddy and happy when he said that (since it's not like anyone's ever said it before), there was still this part of me that wished he could have maybe waited just a little bit longer, told me that just a little bit later. You know, like when Rey would be around to hear it.

By the time we get to Rey's, I'm starting to feel a little nervous, wondering if my cool new friends will be cool enough for Easton. I mean, let's face it, he's definitely one of those hip, seen-it-all, big-city-dweller types, so I think it's pretty obvious that he's used to some pretty urbane, sophisticated stuff.

But he just parks on the street, grabs my hand, and leads me to the front door. And when we go inside he looks around the formally decorated space, and says, "Nice."

We head for the media room, where everyone's hanging out, drinking beer and listening to music, and basically being all quiet and mellow, which of course gives me a whole new set of worries, making me wonder if I somehow oversold this. I mean, on our way over, I think I might have actually referred to this as a "party," which, you know, basically translates to a night of beer drinking, vase breaking, music blaring, neighbor complaining, cop raiding, and just overall teenage debauchery. When actually, from what I can see, this is really more of a "gathering" since everyone's just hanging out, and acting like they aren't even thinking about trashing the place.

So, hoping he's not too disappointed, I introduce him around, then Easton grabs a beer for himself and a bottle of water for me, and we settle onto the deep, cushy love seat.

I twist the top off my water and gaze across the room, noticing how the flat screen on the far wall is showing *Trainspotting*. And even though it's on mute so we can listen to a Led Zeppelin CD instead, I quickly avert my eyes, determined not to see any more of that movie than I already have. I mean, I watched it once before, when my dad rented it on DVD (yup, that's his idea of good family fare), and despite the fact that it was totally tragic, contained a fair amount of heroin shooting, out-of-control puking, and one totally disgusting bathroom scene that gave me the creeps for more than a week, I really did kind of like it. Though I don't need to see it again. So I sip my water, and lean into Easton (but only because the size of the couch pretty much leaves me with no other alternative, and *not* because I'm trying to prove anything to Rey by trying to make him jealous, or anything remotely like that), while everyone's talking about just how scripted and fake reality TV really is, when Shay leans forward, cocks her head to the side, and looking right at Easton and me, says, "Oh, my God, I should take a picture. You guys are *so* adorable together."

And even though I guess in a way that might sound kind of nice, it's actually mostly embarrassing. But I don't tell her that. Instead I just shrug and focus all of my attention on my nasty, shredded cuticles, trying to act like Easton and I are way too cool and secure to even comment on that. But when I do finally look up, I'm just in time to catch Rey staring at Easton.

And then Shay, apparently still dazzled by our unmitigated cuteness, goes, "How'd you guys meet, anyway?"

And I just shrug, leaving the storytelling to Easton who uses all of his well-honed actor skills to tell a much improved, slightly abridged version of my New York adventure, leaving out anything that's either too embarrassing, too personal, or that he wasn't exactly privy to.

And even though his version leaves me looking way more cool and far more daring than I've ever actually been in real life, it's not like I can really stop and enjoy the moment, since I'm so caught up in the way Rey is watching him, almost like he's scrutinizing him, that I can't help but wonder if it's because he feels like a big brother to me, and just wants to be all protective.

Or if maybe, it's something else.

A couple hours later, I'm in a bedroom with Easton. Lying on someone else's bed. Totally making out. And even though my lips are busy kissing his, my mind is busy hoping that this queen-sized bed, with the dark red, silky duvet, and the profusion of beaded pillows does *not* belong to Rey's parents.

Though I am kind of hoping that it might belong to Rey. Because even though that too could be considered kinda gross (in more ways than one), I guess what I'm really hoping is that he'll come strolling in, looking for his favorite childhood model horse (even though I'm fully aware of how that sort of thing only happens on TV and never in real life), when he'll stumble upon us and just stand there in shock, suddenly forced to see me in a whole new light. You know, as someone sexy, desirable, and quite obviously coveted, and not anything like the confused lab partner, reluctant organic sandwich eating, little sister stand-in who needs protection from the big bad Easton like he currently thinks.

And even though I know it's a really terrible thing to be kissing one guy while dreaming about another, it's not like I can actually kiss the guy I'm dreaming about, so what am I supposed to do?

But then, just as Easton tries to snake his hand up my top, I push him away, readjust my clothes, run my hands through my hair, and say, "I'll be right back."

And he just sits up, looks at me, and goes, "Bring me a beer?"

I wander around the house, opening doors and peeking in rooms, fully prepared to stand by my story of how I'm merely looking for a bathroom and *not* searching for Rey, should anyone ask. And it's not until I've pretty much given up on finding him, that I spot him in the kitchen, sans Shay, all hunched over and peeking his head in the fridge.

"Hey." He turns to face me with two bottles of cold beer cradled awkwardly in his arms. "Want one?" he asks, shutting the door with his foot.

Actually, I don't. But Easton does. And since it will give me an opportunity to linger, I nod.

He flips off the top then hands it to me, then we each take a swig and look at each other. And we stay like that for a while, just swigging and looking, until he finally says, "So, Easton seems cool."

I just shrug and take another sip. I mean, yeah, Easton is cool, no doubt about it, but this kind of feels like Rey's digging for information and there's no way I'm giving it up that easy.

And then just as he opens his mouth to say something else, Shay pokes her perfectly beautiful head inside, and says, "Hey baby, what's taking?" And when she sees me she narrows her eyes, and glances suspiciously between us. Rey and me, me and Rey, back and forth again and again, like she's watching a Ping-Pong match.

And even though part of me is excited to see her so suspicious, and even though part of me is glad she's got the wrong idea, I also realize how totally unfair, not nice, and just overall despicable that is. So I grab a bottle of water, mumble good-bye, and head back upstairs to join Easton.

The next morning we're saying good-bye when—oh, yeah, that's right, the *next* morning. You see after a long night of drinking (Easton) and making out (both of us), it was pretty late, and Easton was pretty drunk, and I just couldn't allow him to drive all the way back to L. A., or anywhere else for that matter. And since I'm painfully lacking in any and all of the legal requirements that would allow me to take matters into my own sober hands, we decided just to leave the car on the street, and walk all the way back to my house (well, I walked, Easton just sort of swayed from side to side), where I got him all set up on the couch with two sheets, two pillows, and a thick cotton blanket in case he got cold.

And then I had no choice but to creep into my mom's room, wake her, and tell her all about it. I mean, I just couldn't risk having her totally freak the next morning when she staggered into the kitchen, anticipating a cup of freshly brewed, organic green tea, only to find Easton all hungover and tangled up in multiple layers of natural fiber bedding.

Okay, so I'm standing across the street from Rey's, saying good-bye to Easton, when I happen to turn just in time to see Shay walk out the front door, looking all shiny, showered, and radiant, as she heads down the walkway and onto the street. And I just stand there and gape, my mouth hanging wide-open, when I realize what this means.

Shay and Rey slept together!

And even though I realize that had she actually turned in time to see Easton and I hugging good-bye she probably would have thought the exact same thing, the fact is they *did* and we *didn't*.

I mean, for starters, nothing happened between Easton and me. In fact, if you totaled up all of the times we hooked up (on both coasts), and calculated how far we went, you'd find that it actually totals out somewhere just shy of second base (even though I fully admit that he tried to steal third but I called him out).

But Rey's parents are out of town.

And Shay's parents are out of town.

And her hair was wet. Which means she took a shower. Which also means that at one point, she was actually standing in his house, in his bathroom, completely naked.

So you do the math.

And after forcing myself to drag my gaze away from her, I say good-bye to Easton, and head home in a daze.

But then, for some reason, right when I'm about halfway there, I change my mind and decide to drop by the café instead.

And that's when I run into Sloane.

Sunday, still October, 2006

4:45 P.M.

Current Mood—Melancholy, baby

Current Music—Dark, sad, instrumental jazz ensemble piece

Quote of the Day—"Talk low, talk slow, and don't say too much."—
John Wayne's advice on acting

Stupid Girls

Seen: Approaching the corner of Forest and Ocean, Princess Pink and her Pastel Posse, strolling four wide across the sidewalk, hogging it like they own it.

Me: Just minding my own business, not bothering anyone, while attempting to have a conversation with skinny smoker dude that will hopefully serve as an apology and make up for some of my earlier rudeness.

P. P. and P. P.: "Omigod. Check it out! Loser found herself a boyfriend!" This was followed by laughing, squealing, pointing, eye-rolling, and basically just your everyday show of self-satisfied, girl-on-girl bullying.

So, with that in mind, I guess it's safe to conclude that she no longer feels the need to cry on my shoulder and/or confide in me about her semipublic, dark moment over her dad's seemingly never-ending prison stint.

So in honor of *that,* I give to you, The List:

13. In eighth grade P. P. saved up all of her allowance and birth-day money for a pair of breast-enhancing gel inserts (a.k.a. chicken cutlets), complete with authentic-looking, perfectly

molded, painted-on nipples that she saw in one of her mom's numerous lingerie catalogues. And she was so excited when they finally arrived, that she decided to shove them into her bikini top, and wear them down to the beach that very same day. When she spotted her crush skim boarding nearby, she was so desperate to get his attention, and show off her brand-new, forty-nine ninety-five (plus shipping and handling) boobs, that she grabbed her boogie board and headed for the water, waiting for just the right moment to run by. But her balance wasn't the only thing she lost when she tumbled headfirst into the ocean. And when she finally resurfaced, gasping for air, tangled in seaweed, and choking on saltwater, she had no choice but to watch in horror as her neighbor's golden retriever, Honey Bear, sprinted toward shore, bright green tennis ball long forgotten and quickly replaced by a single gel-filled breast enhancer clenched firmly between his teeth, with perky painted-on nipple slapping the side of his mouth as he raced across the sand, anxious to share this exciting, newfound treasure with his confused and embarrassed owner.

And the other chicken cutlet you ask? Well, that one just bobbed along the Pacific, making its slow, lazy way to Catalina Island.

Sincerely yours,

Eleanor Rigby.

Seventeen

Okay, so the real reason I was talking to skinny smoker dude is because, as it turns out, not only does he own that liquor store, but apparently he's like this semifamous, mad genius, artist, musician guy that is idolized by practically everyone in Laguna Beach and zip codes far beyond.

That is, everyone but me. As apparently I've been way too superficial to get past the back alley nicotine habit to see through to the sensitive soul residing beneath that grungy exterior.

And I happen to know that this local folk hero tale is true because Autumn confirmed it. But that was only after I'd already heard it from Rey, Evan, Elijah, Clark, Hayden, and Shay. Hell, even Easton claimed to have heard of him.

"You didn't know?" Autumn said, her eyes all bugged-out and wide, just like Dakota Fanning when she's acting with all her might.

But I just shrugged. I mean, not only was I feeling kind of

dumb and out-of-the-loop, but I also felt pretty awful for being so shallow that I'd written him off based solely on his appearance. I mean, not only did that point to a glaring lack of imagination on my part, not to mention an embarrassingly heavy reliance on preconceived ideas (which is awful enough on its own), but when you add that to the fact of how so far, I've pretty much spent the sum total of my life being ignored by nearly every kid at school for pretty much the exact same, stupid, shallow, narrow reason, well, that just made it even worse.

So now, I'm lounging on my bed, watching Autumn start yet another new sketch (I swear that kid's prolific), while remembering all the gory details of my encounter with Sloane and fantasizing about revenge scenarios so mean and so sick I couldn't even list them in my blog, when my mom peeks her head in our room and says, "Autumn? Can you leave us alone for a few minutes? I need to talk to your sister."

And when I see the look on her face, I think:

Oh, please God, no. I'll do anything. I'll clean my room, be nicer to Autumn, stop rolling my eyes all the time, but please, not this. Not . . . the Talk!

But despite my silent begging, pleading, and offering up an entire list of potentially false promises that I know I'll never live up to, my mom makes herself comfortable on the end of my bed, clears her throat, looks me right in the eye, and says, "Winter, after you left on your date last night, it hit me just how quickly you're growing up. And I'm afraid I may have been more than a little remiss on explaining a few things that I think you should know."

My eyes glaze over as my lids start to sag with a heaviness that's almost too much to bear. And I'm sure you can guess the rest.

It starts with her being glad that I made the "wise decision" of "not getting into a car with a judgment-impaired and obviously drunk young man." Followed by the fact that she "wasn't born yesterday and realizes that kids are going to experiment." And finally, concluding with "when two young people are very much in love they don't drink, they don't do drugs, and they don't under any circumstances, have sex. Yet, if for some unforeseen reason they *accidentally* do, then they make sure to arm themselves with brand-name, statistically proven, FDA-approved, doctor-endorsed protection that will not only prevent an unwanted pregnancy but also the transmission of any and all STDs."

And unwilling to do anything that might drag this out even longer, I don't say a single word or interrupt in any way. I just nod and smile through the entire tirade, and when it's finally, mercifully over, I remember to thank her as I send her on her way.

Monday at lunch the strangest thing happens. I'm sitting with my friends (yes, I can actually call them that now), and only glancing at those adorable, frisky lovebirds (Sloane and Cash), between occasional bites of my nitrate-free salami sandwich, when Elijah says, "Hey, I came across this new blog the other day."

And of course, the second I hear the word *blog* I instantly perk up, focusing my undivided attention back onto my friends, leaning in a little closer since I'm pretty curious to hear what he has to say on the subject, mostly because I'm always looking for ways to improve mine.

"It's called 'The Gospel of Eleanor Rigby,' or something like that," he says.

"Weird freaking name," Hayden says, pushing her hair out of her face as she bites the end off a baby carrot stick.

And then without even thinking, I go, "Oh, that's from an old Beatles song, you know, from the *Revolver* album." And then the second it's out, I notice how everybody's now looking at me, and I go into a total panic, realizing how I just completely outed myself, and feeling pretty sure that there's basically no way I can ever recover. I mean, let's face it, it's not like anyone my age ever listens to that song, and the only reason *I* even know it is because my mom just happens to be a Beatles freak (big surprise), and their songs pretty much served as the soundtrack for the first seven years of my life. And that's also the reason why I thought it was so perfect, you know? Because it would throw people off the trail of the person who was really behind it (me). It's like, the actual song is about all these lonely people that no one ever notices, not even when they *die!* And that's exactly how I feel sometimes. Like I could just fade away, and nobody would really notice. But now, someone *is* noticing, and I'm not quite sure what to do about it. I mean, I'm such a clueless dork, I even said the album name!

But then Elijah looks at Hayden, rolls his eyes, and goes, "Duh."

Which, sadly, is also his totally retarded, inept way of flirting with her. Since just about everyone at this table knows how he's all in love with her.

But Hayden just shrugs and picks up another baby carrot.

And then Rey goes, "Cool, I'll look for it."

And then Clark goes, "Dude, you better do more than just look for it. You better read it, study it, and learn from it because your blog is getting boring. I mean, puppy training? Come *on*. Nobody wants to read that shit."

I glance at Rey, curious to see how he'll react to that. But when our eyes briefly meet, I quickly look away. And even though I'm feeling pretty good that my secret is still safe, not to mention how I'm apparently not the only one who hates Rey's blog, I just take a bite of my sandwich and nod my head, as though I just might look up old Eleanor Rigby, too.

Eighteen

On Halloween I dress up as that Mia chick that Uma Thurman played in *Pulp Fiction,* while Rey goes as Vincent Vega. Even though Rey's like way thinner, way better-looking, and a whole lot younger than John Travolta. And it feels kind of weird to be dressing up with him like this, since obviously it's pretty much a couple's costume, and in the real world (the one that exists outside of my head) it's not like we're a couple.

Not to mention how the wig that I'm wearing looks exactly like Shay's real hair, which makes me painfully aware of the major differences between her amazingly beautiful face and my amazingly ordinary one. But still, in a kind of sick, sadistic way, it also allows me to imagine what it must feel like to be her. You know, to have hair like that, and to be Rey's girlfriend. And I gotta admit, it feels pretty good, even though I'm fully aware of how at the stroke of the final bell it will all be over. And how tonight she'll be wearing the same exact costume when she also dresses up as Mia and goes to a Sage Hill party with Rey's version of Vincent Vega. A party at which, needless to say, I am so not invited.

But earlier in the week, when we were talking about costumes and trying to come up with ideas that weren't all that obvious, and that only a few, cool, select, in-the-know people would actually recognize, Rey asked me to do him a huge favor and dress up as Mia at school, since absolutely no one would know who he was if he showed up all by himself in an oversized suit, rumpled white shirt, bolo tie, and messy ponytail.

So I agreed. And I fully admit that at first I though it was really fun. Wearing the wig, attaching a fake syringe to my chest, and indulging in this little head game where I pretended that I hadn't completely blown it that night at the club and that Rey and I really were this way cool, superhappy, totally in-love couple.

I mean, isn't that what Halloween is all about? The chance to climb on out of your tiny, narrow, self-made cage, and pretend, at least for a day, that you're someone far more exciting and interesting than you really are?

So I'm at my locker, changing out books, and slowly moving my head back and forth so I can enjoy the feel of that silky, synthetic wig hair as it swings against my cheek, when I see Sloane, Jaci, Holly, and Claire.

Jaci is dressed as a slutty French maid, Holly is in a sexy gypsy costume (which pretty much consists of last year's boho clothes with tons of big, gold jewelry, lots of eye makeup and an inexplicable fake beauty mark that looks a lot like Cindy Crawford's), Claire is a Playboy bunny (which, rumor has it, is actually an authentic costume that was once worn by her mom, or nana, or step-nana or something), and Sloane is a hot mermaid—wearing a freshly sprayed coat of Mystic tan, a tiny bikini top covered in seashells, a dangly, gold, starfish belly ring, and this long, turquoise, sparkly, sequined, fishtail skirt, which is dragging behind her, sweeping the floor and gathering trash, like a really glamorous mop. Along with these super-high, clear plastic stilettos that I happen to know for a fact are leftover from her mom's (not so long ago) "way off-Broadway" dancer days.

And believe it or not, this is actually the other half of a couple's costume. Because just a few hours earlier I spied Cash from across the quad, and did a complete double take when I saw how he was all dressed up as a sailor. And even though I firmly believe that all people should be treated equal, and that whatever someone does in their private life is definitely none of my business, I still have to admit that seeing Cash dressed up like that really did surprise me. I mean, it just bordered so dangerously close on "newest member of the Village People" territory.

But after seeing Sloane, I now know that my earlier suspicions are completely unfounded. I mean, obviously when he's standing by himself, or even worse, next to Andy who's dressed as a cowboy, there was no doubt how it seemed like he (they) were making some sort of startling announcement. But now that I know Sloane's out there, wandering the halls as a mermaid, well, I think we can all agree that his masculinity need no longer be called into question.

And just as I'm thinking all of this Sloane sashays right past me, and actually gazes right at me with no inkling or spark of recognition whatsoever. And I smile when I realize how today *she's* the one who's not cool enough, hip enough, or select enough, to know *me*.

I close my locker and turn to follow (well, not exactly *follow,* but like, I have no choice but to head in that same direction if I want to get to my next class on time), when I notice there's something stuck to the back of her mermaid skirt, right smack-dab in the middle of her ass. And how not one of her new best friends seem to think it necessary to point out this little fact to her. Even though I'm pretty sure they've all seen it (especially since Sloane tends to walk just slightly ahead of them at all times).

So I pick up the pace, trying not to be too obvious about the fact that, yes, I am now officially stalking her. And just as I start to gain ground, I sort of lean in and squint at this little yellow Post-it note that's stuck to her mermaid butt.

And then my eyes bug out, and my jaw drops in shock when I see that it says, "I Love Seamen!" Only there's a big red slash through the *a*.

Then I just smile and waltz right past her, secure in the knowledge that the war's already started.

THE GOSPEL OF ELEANOR RIGBY

November ??, 2006
7:45 P.M.
Current Mood—Happy like you can't even believe
Current Music—That song where Bono counts to 14
Quote of the Day—"For a good cause, wrongdoing is virtuous."
—Pubilius Syrus

God Save the Queen

Someone is sabotaging Princess Pink. Sticking nasty notes on her butt, defacing her locker, scribbling on bathroom walls, spreading rumors, and even revealing some of her newer secrets that, for obvious reasons, I haven't exactly been privy to. And the culprits are so damn obvious I can hardly believe how clueless she remains. Though of course I would be more than willing to enlighten her and give her the heads-up she so desperately needs, if only she didn't deserve it quite so much.

But then, that's one of the advantages to being me. I mean, you can see everything when you're invisible.

And now, The List:

14. After getting to first base with her first cousin, the very next week Princess Pink decided to run for second when they were interrupted by his mom (her aunt). When they simply explained how they were just "practicing" for some future time when it will "really matter," auntie left the room, and they got back to it.

15. P. P. has had her Spring Break nose job booked for more than a year now, it's one of her sweet sixteen birthday presents

(her other present, no doubt, will be a brand-new Mercedes SLK or its equivalent). But even though P. P. is destined to show off the second gift to anyone who will look, she's planning to lay pretty low on the first. Having spent the better part of the summer working on an elaborate story of how she'll be tucked away in some luxurious condo, somewhere in the mountains of Colorado. But don't you believe it when she shows up on the first day back wearing her sky-blue "Ski Aspen!" T-shirt. Her mom ordered it off the Internet more than six months ago.

16. I can solemnly swear that the last time I was in her room, Princess Pink was still sleeping with her much adored, slightly stinky, Nick Lachey pillowcase cover (and yelling at the maid every time she tried to wash it). While insisting that I call her "Mrs. Lachey" for the first two weeks following the big divorce announcement.

Au revoir,

Eleanor Rigby

Nineteen

My dad's gonna be on TV. Or rather, he's *thinking* about being on TV. Apparently, some cable channel is planning a reality show tentatively titled "Act II" about a group of former stars who've moved on to something a little bigger and better than repeated Betty Ford rehab stints or mug shot posing in the Smoking Gun Hall of Fame.

And even though I'm still undecided on how I really feel about all of this, I mean, part of me is going, "TV!" While the other part is going, "TV?" The thing is, my dad is actually considering it. In fact he's more than considering it, he's actually moving forward with the plan, having already gathered a team of lawyers, agents, stylists, and publicists who are poring over every last detail on that proposed contract. And the last time we spoke he happened to mention that if all went well, then he was just days away from signing.

And after listening to all of that, and forcing myself to try and get used to the idea before rushing to judgment, I finally just took a deep breath and voiced all of my concerns, at which point he did his best to assure me that:

1. He would do everything in his power *not* to embarrass me on national television.

2. It will be great exposure for the gallery, by really getting the name out there (not to mention his name) to a whole new group of people.

3. It will be great exposure for the artists that are shown in the gallery, as it will help to build their names and therefore their careers (as well as his).

4. "I'm getting paid for this, Winter, and while I won't disclose how much, let me just say that it's definitely worth my while. Excuse me, make that worth *our* while." (As though I'm getting a cut or something.)

But the worst part came when he actually sums it all up by adding:

5. "And who knows where all this will lead?"

And it's *that* which got me all worried. It's the "who knows" part that really made my skin crawl.

Because the truth is, I *know* he's dreaming of a rock-and-roll comeback. I mean, how could he not? And while I totally want him to be happy, and live his dreams, and all that peaceful, well-wishing, good karma, blah blah blah stuff, the whole idea of my dad getting another shot at the music video filming, magazine cover posing, out-of-control rock star life kinda makes me cringe. I mean, *hello,* he's like forty-one for God's sake! And the thought of him tying a silk scarf to his microphone, leaping around stage in too-tight pants, and partying afterward with a harem of Playboy mansion groupies (who are probably closer to my age than his) just totally creeps me out.

I mean, why can't I just have normal parents like everyone else? Why can't they just blend in and try a little harder to assimilate into the *real world*. The one we're *all* forced to live in. And *not* the one they invent as they go along.

Why do they insist on standing out *so freaking much*?

And then, the other day at school, I was in the bathroom between classes, reaching for a paper towel, when I noticed that right there on the wall in front of me someone had written: "Sloane loves to" (do something so completely dirty I can't possibly repeat it here).

So not only am I wondering which member of the princess posse carries a fine black Sharpie in her Gucci tote bag for the sole purpose of freely expressing herself whenever the inspiration strikes, but also if it's true what they wrote about Sloane and her (alleged) new hobby.

And as if that wasn't enough, I also heard via Hayden (who knows way more gossip than I ever would have guessed, and is not afraid to repeat it), that Rey and Shay are headed for a major blowout and/or breakup (that is, if they're not there already). Apparently Shay got pretty upset when she saw the photos we took at school, and how I was all dressed up as Mia. Which, of course, I also realize, is something that a truly good friend would never, ever, even consider gloating about.

But there you have it.

"So, what're you doing tonight?" Rey asks, peering at me from over the top of his Dietrich's cup, like he already has something in mind.

We're on our way to school, and I'm thinking how weird it is that Evan never joins us in the mornings, you know, since he's always around when we're walking home. But it probably has a lot more to do with the fact that Evan's dad drops him off on his way to work, than Rey secretly cherishing this early A.M. alone time with me.

I glance at Rey, who's patiently waiting for a response, but I just shrug. I mean, now that Easton is out of the picture and back in New York, I'm done playing games, and trying to act as though I'm coveted.

"Listen, I'm auditioning this potential drummer for the band I'm trying to put together, and since my parents are away again, I've decided to do it at my house. So I was wondering if you'd maybe want to stop by and listen in? You know, check it out and tell me what you think?"

And while he's wondering that, I'm wondering if Shay will be there. And it's not like I'm not dying to just come out and ask, but somehow I just can't allow myself to risk being that obvious about it. So I just shrug and go, "Sounds good." And then, "Um, you wanna do something after, or do you have plans with Shay?" I know, totally lame, but still direct and to the point.

But he just rolls his eyes and shakes his head, and since he seems kind of upset when he does that, I turn away so he can't see me smile.

Hayden is the exact opposite of Sloane. I mean, where Sloane's all fluffy and trendy and cute and super-(fake) sweet (well, to everyone but me), Hayden is slick and edgy and kind of sarcastic, which is a lot like me. Only she's way cooler than me. And by lunch when I realize that Rey has pretty much asked *everyone* to stop by his house to check out the potential new drummer (which leaves me feeling like an idiot for pretending like he was asking me on a date, when obviously it's just some group endeavor to vote on a drummer), Hayden turns to me and asks if I want to maybe grab a bite beforehand.

And I just nod, trying to act cool, since I've never actually hung out with just her before. You know, one-on-one, without all the guys. And I was actually starting to wonder it it's because she doesn't like me.

So we agreed to meet at this cool, little, independent record store that specializes in punk. And even though I felt pretty secure that I actually knew a thing or two about punk (especially since my mom *hates* punk, I mean, seriously hates it. Like, so bad that just seconds after learning that, I immediately pledged my undying devotion to Sid Vicious, Johnny Rotten, and all the other members of the Sex Pistols), after browsing through titles I've never even heard of, by bands I didn't even know existed, I'm suddenly starting to realize that owning one copy of *Never Mind the Bullocks* just to freak out my mom, does not a punk devotee make.

So after looking around the store, I head over to where Hayden is and then I just stand there and wait while she wraps up her conversation with the multi-pierced, yet completely hot employee guy. Then we both head out the door and over to this funky outdoor eatery where, once again, she knows just about everyone.

I save us a seat, while she goes inside to order, and as I'm waiting I start thinking about how nice it is to hang out with a girl again, and how I didn't really realize, until now, just how much I missed that kind of female bonding stuff. I mean, as great as Rey is, there's just certain things I can't talk to him about because of the very fact that he's a guy. Not to mention that he's a guy who I also happen to kind of like.

When I look up, I see Hayden heading toward me with these two huge plates piled with tacos and beans, along with a basket of chips and salsa for us to share, and then she sets them on the table, sits across from me, and without any attempt at small talk or beating around the bush, she just looks me right in the eye and goes, "Okay, so what's up with you and Rey?"

And even though just a few seconds ago I may have been looking forward to bonding with her, I definitely don't want to bond over *this*. So I just stare at her. And then I go, "Huh?" like I have no idea what she could possibly be talking about. And then I shrug. And then I pick up one of my tacos and take a bite, chewing slowly and buying time, while my mind races ahead, wondering just how much she knows, and just why exactly it is that she's asking.

But she just gives me this "I'm so not buying you" look, shakes her head, and goes, "Forget it."

And just as I'm about to say, "No, really, please continue, ask me again, go ahead, elaborate if you must," Evan, Elijah, and Clark appear, along with some guy named Mick who, from the bummed-out expression on Elijah's face and the elated one on Hayden's, is most likely her boyfriend. And as he sits down beside her, grabs one of her tacos, and starts talking about the strict, scary, military school his parents are threatening to send him to just because he's getting a C in trig, I glance quickly at Elijah, who looks totally depressed, and think, *Dude, I know just how you feel.*

Apparently, Shay was supposed to sing backup. Or at least fill in 'til Rey got around to auditioning others. But since she's now apparently persona non grata around here (or at the very least, failed to show up), Rey looks from Hayden to me and goes, "Okay, so who's it gonna be?"

So I take the opportunity to point at the guys and go, "Well, what about them?"

But Rey just laughs and says, "Mick's already on guitar, and Clark, Evan, and Elijah suck. Besides, we need a girl voice."

Then Hayden shakes her head and goes, "Don't look at me."

And since I'm the only other girl left in the room, everyone turns to look at me. Then Rey goes, "Well, your dad rocks, so maybe you inherited some of that."

And then everyone looks at me again and goes, "Huh?"

But I just shrug and head for the setup. I mean, I really don't like to talk about my dad and his fifteen minutes of fame.

So after surviving a toned-down, abbreviated, warbled version of "Won't Get Fooled Again," which other than being hugely ambitious for a fledgling band, also happens to be one of the few songs I know every single nuance of since my parents practically piped it into my crib when I was a baby (I mean, most girls are raised on Cinderella rescue fantasies, so that they can grow up believing that Prince Charming is just one perfect pair of Jimmy Choo's away, while Autumn and I were taught cautionary tales of war, political oppression, and dire warnings about "the Man"), Rey comes over and hugs me and goes, "You're in."

And I just stand there, eyes closed, completely enveloped in his arms, enjoying the feel of being so close to him. And even though I really don't want to be "in," it's not like I tell him that. I mean, if nothing else it will give me a really good excuse to hang with him even more than I already do.

Wednesday, November, heading straight into thx-giving, 2006

7:48 P.M.

Current Mood—Been better

Current Music—White Stripes

Quote of the Day- "80 percent of success is showing up."
　　　　　—Woody Allen

Get Behind Me Satan

So, maybe it's evil, but I gotta admit just how enjoyable it's been watching Princess Pink continue to hang out with the very people who are sabotaging her (Pastel Posse), while gazing suspiciously at everyone else. So far, she's endured Post-its on her butt, slander on the bathroom walls (then again, it ain't slander if it's true and since that's yet to be determined . . .), the words "I Love Me" and "I'm a Slut" scrawled across her locker, and my very own personal favorite—a totally bogus MySpace page that displays an old, completely unflattering picture of her that was taken way before she became glamorous and popular, and that proclaims her love of hairy old men with super-long, crusty yellow toenails, confides how she can't wait to buy K. Fed's new CD, and reveals how she's thinking about converting to Scientology so she can finally meet TomKat and possibly babysit for baby Suri.

And even though it's all been admittedly fun to watch, the not-so-fun part is that I'm pretty sure she thinks the culprit is *me.* Because now that someone has stepped up the hate campaign, it's pretty obvious that she's stepped up hers against me. And I guess what it all comes down to in the end, is motive. And even though I think it's painfully clear how there's one particular member of her posse who so did not appreciate getting demoted to second in line when P. P. became the most popular girl in school the instant she hooked up with Captain World, apparently that's not so clear to P. P.

And because of that, she's started waging this kind of low-key campaign against me. Recruiting all of her minions to start up the same old stuff I thought was long over. You know, like "accidentally" bumping into me in the hall, "accidentally" tripping me in class, and "accidentally" saying really mean, superderogatory things to me when I walk by.

And with that in mind, here it is, **The List:**

17. Princess Pink is a big fan of the three-second rule, and apparently does not draw the line at public toilets. We were at the mall, in the bathroom, and right before she flushed I heard a splash (not what you think), followed by, "Oh, well." And when she came out she was carrying a tube of lip gloss, all dripping wet with toilet water, which she then proceeded to dry off with a paper towel, as opposed to: (*a*) throwing it away, or (*b*) scrubbing it clean with a whole lot of antibacterial soap and scalding hot water, and then throwing it away. And so, still damp with bowl juice, she proceeded to twist off the top and glop it onto her lips, completely ignoring the fact of how she'd just retrieved it *from the toilet.*

18. P. P. doesn't like to waste time in the morning by visiting the toilet when she can just relieve herself in the shower and kill two birds with one stone. "What's the big deal?" she asks. "It all ends up in the same place!" Um, yeah, like a puddle up around your feet?

19. In junior high, we were hanging in the food court at the Mission Viejo Mall drinking Cokes and sharing fries, when P. P. spotted her crush. She was so busy watching him that when she leaned down to take a sip of her drink she

missed her mouth and the straw wedged so far up her
nose it required several yanks from me, mall security, and
eventually, a paramedic, to dislodge it, while her grossed-
out crush looked on.

Adios amigos,

Eleanor Rigby

Twenty

Things are getting weird, and I'm not sure what to do about it. I mean, on the surface everything looks great—I've got a new group of friends, I'm not fighting with Autumn as much, my dad's preparing to go on TV (and I've actually made peace with it), and I'm finally starting to feel more comfortable with my role as backup singer in our new band, Social Exile.

But on the other hand, my mom has started dating (yes, of course I'm happy for her, but that doesn't mean I'm not still a little freaked-out, since it seems like *I'm* the one who should be dating, and we all know that I'm not), not to mention how Rey is back with Shay (which I don't think requires any further explanation).

And then, just to put me even more on edge, the other day, in the middle of the five free minutes between fifth and sixth period, I passed Sloane in the hall, and not only did she not trip me, scowl at me, bump into me, or curse at me, but she actually looked me right in the eye and nodded in a way that could definitely be defined as a nonthreatening way of acknowledging my presence. And then, as if that wasn't enough, she continued to look me right in the eye as she opened her frosty pink mouth to say, "Hey."

And even though to the uninformed observer this may appear as just another completely benign greeting, I think by now we all know better. And I was caught so off-guard that I can't remember smiling, waving, nodding, or doing anything that could remotely qualify as acknowledging her back. Though later, when I came to my senses, I realized that this seemingly innocent exchange could only mean one of three things:

1. The Table A sabotage is moving along a lot quicker than I realized (since I admit to sometimes being a little preoccupied with Rey, and not as focused on her as I should be), and now she's actually wondering if her enemy just might be *them* and *not* me, and so she is actively seeking an emergency backup friend just in case the whole thing blows.

2. She's slumming for votes as sophomore class Ice Queen (or whatever the hell they call the tiara wearer at that overblown wingding they call Winter Formal), and wants it so bad she'll even deign to acknowledge me in hopes of a vote.

3. She suffered a recent blow to the head, has been diagnosed with amnesia, and now says "hey" to everyone she comes across, just to cover her bases.

And then just as my plate is really starting to overflow, the very next day I discover that the blog is getting even bigger than I ever could have imagined.

I was at my locker, just changing out my textbooks and

minding my own business, when these three girls, standing just two lockers over, start talking about The List, speculating about who it might be, and wondering what kind of sick, demented person would make out with their own cousin.

I just stood there, frozen stiff, I mean seriously unable to move or do anything other than pretend I wasn't listening, until the bell finally rang and sent them scattering off to class.

And then later when I was at Rey's, and we were taking a break between sets, Pete, the drummer, goes, "Oh, man, did you read number thirteen? So sick!"

So Shay (a.k.a. the permanent groupie who hangs around more than ever now), goes, "Omigod, don't tell me. I just started reading it and I haven't gotten that far yet."

And I just sit there sipping my water, and acting all calm and normal, while feeling completely amazed that people are actually requesting spoiler alerts. Which, truth to be told, actually makes me feel pretty excited. I mean, who would have thought that anyone would even read my blog, much less talk about it?

But then I start to think about Sloane, and how I'm exposing all of her dirty little secrets for the whole world to read, and I start to panic. I mean, even though I still think it's pretty safe to assume that she hasn't seen any of it yet, considering how she's not so big on reading anything that spans more than a page and a half and doesn't contain a beauty tip, a diet tip, and/or a corresponding color photograph of at least one of her favorite celebs. Not to mention how if she had actually read it, I sincerely doubt she'd be nodding at me in the halls and saying "hey," no matter how bad she wants to be Ice Queen.

But still, just because she hasn't read it *yet,* doesn't mean she won't be scrolling through it sometime in the near future, especially if enough people at school start talking about it. And I have no idea what I'll do if that happens.

So we've been practicing almost every other day, and we've even come up with a list of almost twelve pretty solid cover tunes that are a decent representation of the last thirty years in music, and which, thankfully, does *not* include our mangled version of "Won't Get Fooled Again" since we were smart enough to scrap that early on. And even though Rey's got some pretty cool originals that we like to practice now and then, the fact is, most people just want to hear songs that they already know all the words to, so if you plan on playing for your peers, you've pretty much got to nail a few crowd-pleasers.

But the thing is, even though all this practicing has actually been kind of fun, I mean, it's a good excuse to hang with Rey (even if Shay's pretty much always there, too), and it really doesn't require much more from me other than a lot of standing around and gossiping with Hayden since most the songs don't even require a female backup singer, the truth is I'm still kind of unclear on just what exactly the point is. I mean, are we going for the big record deal? Hoping for an American Idol battle of the bands? Booking gigs on the Bar Mitzvah circuit?

It's like, we're pouring all this time and energy into all of these songs, and yet nobody's ever made any mention of just exactly what it is we're doing here, or what exactly it is that we're trying to accomplish. We put in countless hours, rush our homework, and basically go to all kinds of trouble building a catalogue of songs that, from the looks of it, nobody outside of this room will ever actually hear.

And even though I'm fully aware that the only reason I'm here is so I can have a valid reason to hang with Rey after school without causing any undue suspicions, that doesn't begin to address the question of just what the heck everyone else is up to.

And then, wouldn't you know it, just as I'm pondering all of this, I mean just right out of nowhere, Rey looks at us, with his face set all serious when he goes, "People, I think we're finally ready for the talent show."

And since we're not exactly a group of joiners who get all happy with school-sponsored activities (I mean, if you add all of us together you'll come up with three different high schools and not one attended dance or football game among us), and since my last foray into a talent showcase resulted in parental outrage and a threatened suspension, I instinctively cross my arms, shake my head, and go, "Uh-uh. No way. Forget it."

But Rey's not budging. And since he's the one who put this band together in the first place, everyone pretty much recognizes him as the leader.

But no way am I bowing to that kind of dubious, non-voted-on authority, so I just continue to stand there, refusing to budge. Because even though I fully admit that school is no longer the nightmare it used to be, there's still no way I'm getting up onstage in front of Princess Pink and her Pastel Posse so that they can heckle, snicker, sneer, and laugh, while they scrounge around for stuff to throw at us.

Uh-uh. No way. Forget it.

But Rey just looks at me and goes, "Get used to it, Winter, we're going on."

Then he picks up the mike and heads into a semi-rockin' rendition of "American Idiot."

Today is my sixteenth birthday. But it's also Thanksgiving Day. Which, believe me, sucks even more than you can imagine. I mean, not only are all of my friends out of town with their families, busy enjoying the long holiday weekend in some exotic locale, but if you think being presented with a big, brown, one hundred percent organic, undercooked pumpkin pie masquerading as a birthday cake (and also acting as quicksand for the sixteen rapidly sinking candles that have been shoved in the middle), is remotely festive, well, think again.

And as if that wasn't bad enough, my mom has somehow gotten the idea that this is the perfect opportunity to unwrap her new boyfriend and present him to us. Who, don't get me wrong, we've technically met before, but still, up until today our contact has mostly consisted of a brief hello, followed five minutes later by a somewhat awkward good-bye. I guess what I'm trying to say is that up until now he's never actually attended one of our formal (well, formal for us) family gatherings, so this is actually kind of a big deal. But it also makes me wonder why she had to choose today, as opposed to some other day, when it's not actually my birthday.

So it's basically me, Autumn, my mom, and her boyfriend, Dave, and we're all sitting around the dining-room table, with my birthday pie placed prominently before me. And they're all gazing at me with this look of anticipation and excitement, and then completely simultaneously, as though they'd been rehearsing it for weeks, they go, "Make a wish!"

And as I gaze at these sixteen candles, I know I have about five seconds to accomplish this task before they're swallowed up completely.

So I close my eyes, lean in, and think, *Rey, Shay, Sloane, the talent show, the blog, my mom . . .* and all these words and names just jumble together, rushing through my head in no particular order or sequence, and with no real wish attached—like a grocery list written on the fly.

And then Autumn goes, "Hurry up and blow! They're totally sinking!"

So I do. I lean in and blow with all my might. And by the time I open my eyes again, I see that my mom's already retrieving them, licking the tips of her fingers to protect her skin from the smoldering wicks.

And then I watch as she takes her index finger, the one covered in gloppy pumpkin pie chunks, and offers it to Dave's lips so that he can lick it off. And as I'm looking at this, I realize I should be feeling way more grossed-out than I am. But the truth is, I'm actually focused on the whole candle-blowing gig, and how I'm now hoping and praying that there's absolutely no validity to any of that supposed magic whatsoever. That it actually amounts to no more than just another one of those old, played-out, urban myths. You know, like Santa and his elves, the Easter bunny, and that fairy who pays you by the tooth.

Because with a wish list as random and nonspecific as mine, I'm afraid I've just inadvertently put myself in a very vulnerable position. I mean, by failing to define just what exactly it is that I want, I've left the whole thing pretty wide-open, serving as a sort of free-for-all where just about anything can happen!

But now, watching as my mom sticks her finger in her mouth, presumably to lick off any pumpkin morsels that Dave has left behind, I'm still so freaked about the wish that I'm just not as disturbed by that as I should be. So I push all paranoid thoughts out of my head and smile at my mom as she cuts the first piece of pie, then I force myself to look at Dave and admit that he's not nearly as bad as I suspected or feared.

In fact, he's actually sort of nice.

But since my mom really hasn't dated since the divorce (or at least not to my knowledge), I guess I've pretty much always pictured her with some kind of embarrassing, skinny, heavily bearded, eco-freak guy. You know, like the kind who drives an old, beat-up, rusted-out car covered in political bumper stickers, who never leaves home without his moldy Birkenstocks, and who, no matter what the season, is always sporting a glaringly white vegetarian pallor to go with his permanent affliction of bad tofu breath.

But Dave's nothing like that. I mean, he's normal, tan (probably because he surfs every morning), with kind eyes, a nice smile, and a pretty cool, easygoing personality. Also, he's an architect. Which I think is like a pretty cool profession. And even though I'm kind of shocked that my mom would date someone who makes a living, as a sort of "land rapist" (her pre-Dave words, not mine), putting up buildings where bunnies once multiplied and wildflowers swayed happily in the breeze, I guess she thinks it's okay now, because he's "green." Which means he builds in a responsible, earth-sustaining, ecologically sound kind of way.

So after eating a piece of my b-day pie and opening all of my presents, which consisted of three gift cards (Barnes & Noble and Urban Outfitters from my mom, Sephora from Dave), and a supercool necklace that Autumn made and that I'm actually already wearing (and not just out of familial loyalty but because I really do like it), I excuse myself and go to my room, because I kind of want to be by myself for a while so I can read some of the comments that people have posted on my blog.

And as I log on and scroll through them, I'm amazed at how many people have something to say about the goings-on in my day-to-day life. And even though seeing all of this makes me feel kind of happy, popular, and cool (and even, I admit, a little bit famous), I'm also growing increasingly worried about getting caught. Not to mention how I'm starting to feel the building of some serious pressure to come up with even bigger and better stuff. You know, like juicier secrets, and more examples of Sloane's awfulness.

Because from what I've already gathered by reading just a few of these comments, this is one outspoken, highly opinionated, bloodthirsty crowd. And they've made it painfully clear how not a single one of them appreciated the more mundane secrets, or anything to do with junior high farting incidents or shower peeing, which apparently, is way more common than I would've thought.

It's like these readers are so desensitized, so impatient, and so overexposed to sensational tabloid headlines that scream stuff about heiress porn, dehydrated starlets, and all manner of celebrity couch-jumping antics, that nothing short of the big scandalous story will do.

Which is fine for them. And it's not like I'm judging or anything as even I've been mesmerized by the shocking sight of telephoto-lens-captured celebrity cellulite, wondering if it was actually real. But the fact is, I *don't* work for the *Enquirer*. Not to mention how I'm just an ordinary sixteen-year-old girl from small-town America (yes, Laguna Beach is a small town, population 24,000, thank you very much), who just felt the need to vent a little, and yeah, I admit, get some good, old-fashioned, healthy, yet well-deserved revenge on a former friend who done me wrong.

But now I'm starting to wonder if maybe, just maybe, I've gotten in a little too deep.

And if so, then I also have to admit that I really don't have the slightest clue how to get out.

I mean, sure I could just close up shop and blog no more. But the thing is, I promised these people the whole story, the unmitigated, fact-based truth. So I really can't see how quitting right smack in the middle is in any way a valid option. It's like, if nothing else, I like to think that I'm a person who makes good on my word (unlike Sloane). And yes, even though I realize how that may, on the surface at least, seem really hypocritical, since obviously it's not like I'm standing by my word when I expose all of her secrets, the fact is, that after what she did to me I now firmly believe that any former obligation or loyalty to her has become sort of null and void. Besides, I really think that once I've said my piece and am winding down, the whole thing will lose steam, my readers will be more or less satiated, and everyone will just click over to the next big thing. And I promise, that once that happens I will happily close up shop, and quietly fade into blog oblivion.

But until that day arrives, I definitely feel the need to come up with some major juice, or suffer at the hands of some very angry readers.

And just as I'm about to log off, Autumn walks in, takes one look at the screen, and goes, "Oh, jeez, don't tell me you're into that, too? Everyone at school is talking about it."

And when I turn and look at her, I concentrate on keeping

my expression calm and serene, because deep down inside, my heart is hammering, my palms are sweating, and it pretty much feels as though my entire nervous system has gone into crisis mode.

"*A lot* of speculation on who it might be," she continues, getting onto her hands and knees and retrieving her art portfolio out from under her bed.

"But that's ridiculous," I say, frantically staring at the back of her head. "I mean, it could be about anyone, from anywhere."

But Autumn just shakes her head, sits on her bed, and starts flipping through her drawings. "Nope, it's definitely local," she says, not even looking at me.

"What makes you so sure?" I ask, trying to sound sort of neutral, and only mildly interested.

"Well, for starters, did you read the one where she talks about skinny smoker dude? I mean, hello, there's only one of those that I know of."

I just laugh. I mean, if this is the only evidence she can come up with, then I'm starting to feel pretty good about my prospects for keeping my anonymity intact. So I just roll my eyes and go, "Autumn, that's insane. I'm sure there's a skinny smoker dude on practically every corner, in every downtown area, in every city in America, if not the entire world!"

But she just shrugs, finds the picture she's looking for, and carries it out of the room. While I frantically scroll back through all of my entries, wondering how on earth I could've been so careless.

Twenty-one

I'm going to hell. No, seriously. Got myself a one-way ticket, nonstop, nonrefundable, and definitely nonnegotiable. And I feel so awful about the reason why, that I'm actually pretty reluctant to share it.

Though I do think it's safe to say that during the short amount of time it took to engage in the "why" I wasn't exactly feeling all that bad about it.

In fact, it was pretty much the exact opposite.

It was only later, when I got caught, that I started to suffer.

It was the Sunday evening following my birthday (or Thanksgiving Day, whichever is more important to you), and I went over to Rey's because he just got back from his family's place in Napa Valley. And after saying hello to his parents, he led me into the media room, where he got this big smile on his face as he presented me with this small, thin, shiny, wrapped package.

"Happy birthday," he said, handing it to me.

I slipped my nail stub under the transparent tape and re-moved the navy-blue paper, where I found a red plastic jewel case containing a homemade, compilation CD, and some pretty impressive cover art that I recognized immediately as Rey's. And after standing there for a moment, turning it over in my hand and reading each side, I smiled shyly, and said, "Um, thanks. This is so sweet of you."

Then he took it from me and said, "First you gotta hear it." He slid it into the stereo, pushed Play, and just stood there smiling as the room filled with the sound of Social Exile (sans moi) doing an amazing rendition of "A Hazy Shade of Winter" (which if you'll remember, is the exact same song he sang to me in Dietrich's that day). Only this time he got all the lyrics right.

I just stood very still, listening to the song, and slowly re-alizing how Rey had arranged it all just for me, just because it was my birthday. And when it finally ended, I felt so wildly happy and elated, yet also kind of embarrassed and unsure of what to do next. I mean, even though I wanted it to mean something big, the fact was, I was painfully aware of how he was still with Shay. Which basically meant that this gift prob-ably didn't mean near as much to him as it did to me. And that it was probably just another recorded jam session, in a succes-sion of many, and therefore was never meant to be a big deal.

And fully aware of how I needed to just relax and stay very cool about the whole thing or risk outing my true feelings, I just looked right at him and said, "Oh, that's so cool. Thanks."

Then I leaned in to hug him.

Which, if you think about it, is really not such a big deal since that's what people usually do when someone gives them a gift. Besides, it's not like we hadn't ever hugged before.

But this time, as I pulled away, our eyes accidentally met, and the next thing I knew, we were kissing. And I don't mean some little grandma-style peck on the cheek. I'm talking about real-deal, full-blown, Hollywood-love-scene kissing. And it was so perfect. So seriously awesome. And his hands were all buried in my hair, and mine were wrapped around his neck, and even while it was happening I could hardly believe that it was really happening, because it was just that amazing.

But then someone came into the room, cleared their throat, and said, "Excuse me."

And the second we broke apart, I turned toward the door and saw Shay.

"Happy birthday," she said, throwing a small wrapped box at me, aiming for my head, and only missing by a fraction.

I just stood there, staring at the silver box with the curly purple ribbon lying at my feet, feeling like the most horrible person on the entire planet, as she ran crying from the room.

Then Rey yelled, "Shay! Oh, man. Wait!"

And as he went running after her, I picked up the gift, set it on the table, and let myself out.

And on Monday morning, I quit the band.

"Forget it. You can't quit," Rey says, shaking his head and looking at me.

"But I just did." I shrug, taking a sip of my coffee.

He leans toward me, elbows on the table, eyes fixed on mine. "Listen, believe it or not, we worked it out. She's mad and all, don't get me wrong, but that's my problem, not yours. So don't worry about it. It's handled."

I glance at him briefly, then look away. I mean, doesn't he get it? Doesn't he know that's exactly the reason I'm quitting? Because now that we've had that amazing kiss, I can no longer sit around and act like I don't care when *they* kiss. It's like, there's just no way on earth I can go through all that again. In fact, little does he know, but not only am I quitting the band, but I'm also quitting the lunch table. And after today, these early-morning coffee meetings will be history, too. Only I don't tell him any of that. He'll find out soon enough.

"Winter," he says, his eyes pleading with me.

But I just grab my coffee and stand. "Come on, we're gonna be late for school," I say, heading for the door.

Twenty-two

My dad is famous. Again. And this time he's got not only the numbers to back it up, but also the reviews:

TV Addict magazine says, "*Act II* is primetime's newest guilty pleasure!"

TiVo Times exclaims, "*Act II* is endlessly watchable!"

Reality Recap reveals, "Finally, some real-life people worth rooting for!"

My mother gasps, "Oh, my God, what is your father doing?"

And then the day after my dad's stunning reality TV debut, I step on campus and within seconds it's clear that word is out. Which means that my dad is also out—or at least no longer a secret. And it's not that anyone actually says anything directly *to* me, it's more the way they all look *at* me as I walk around campus. And the way they nudge one another when I stroll into class. I mean, let's face it, it wasn't all that long ago that I was completely invisible to practically everyone other than Clark, Evan, Elijah, Hayden, and Rey. Hell, even Sloane acted like she no longer knew me. So the mere fact that I'm suddenly attracting any kind of notice is pretty much all I need to justify my suspicions. And since I'm well aware of how I've done nothing to elicit this kind of attention, I've got to believe it's my dad who's to thank for all this.

But later, right after lunch, when I actually overhear a group of freshmen girls singing the opening lines to my dad's hit song, "Gobsmacked" (which also serves as the show's theme song), it suddenly dawns on me that the only people in this entire school who could actually connect me to my dad are Rey and Sloane. I mean, let's face it, Simmons is not exactly considered to be an exotic, unusual, or in any way extraordinary last name. So if it was that alone that prompted all of these people to suddenly take notice of me then why wouldn't they have noticed me before, wondering if I'm quite possibly the offspring of Gene Simmons, Richard Simmons, or Simmons Beauty Rest mattress?

So, by following this logic, I'm pretty convinced that this sudden rush of attention most likely stems from the loose lips of either Rey or Sloane. Because like I said, they're the only ones who know. Which makes one of them responsible.

Though it's not like I'm about to confront them or anything, I mean, what good would it do? What's done is done. And other than seventh-period chemistry class where we pretty much have no choice but to work as lab partners, Rey and I really don't talk anymore. And it took a solid week of him trying to talk to me before he finally got the hint and gave up.

So now we keep all of our brief conversations as professional, businesslike, and to the point as possible. Relegating ourselves to phrases like:

"Can you pass me that beaker, please?"

Or, "Don't forget to light that Bunsen burner."

And because of that, my life has become a lot simpler.

Which means I've pretty much convinced myself that whatever happened that night in the media room is no longer an issue. Not at all important. And in no way relevant to how I'm currently living my life.

And then, as I'm walking home from school, by myself (even though I know for a fact that Rey and Evan are right directly behind me), I stop at the next corner and wait for the light to change just as Cash Davis pulls up in his big, shiny, black Hummer with his picture-perfect princess (Sloane) sitting right alongside him.

And believe me, like the second I realize it's them, I just stare straight ahead, my eyes unwavering on a spot far, far away, pretending like I've no idea they're stopped right there beside me. And just as the light turns green and I step off the curb, Sloane slides down her window, sticks her head out, and goes, "Hey! Winter! Omigod, I didn't even see you! Do you need a ride?"

I stop in the middle of the street, looking at her and thinking:

1. Is she serious?
2. If she's serious, then what the heck is she up to?
3. This may be just the opportunity I need to build up the blog with some up-close-and-personal inside investigating.

So I smile, nod, and climb into the back, making myself comfortable on the long bench seat. And as Cash pulls away from the curb, I glance quickly at Rey and Evan, just to see their expression. And when my eyes briefly meet Rey's, well, "shocked" is probably the best way to describe him.

"So, how've you been?" Sloane asks, turning in her seat and smiling at me like the well-trained, well-mannered, gracious hostess that six-week finishing school last spring taught her to be. Acting as though we're just two old friends, who through no fault of hers simply lost touch.

And I, automatically assuming my full-on investigative reporter mode, start noting all the little details while nodding and smiling and just basically following her lead. "I'm great," I tell her. "And you?"

I watch as she flips her long blond hair over her shoulder, glances at Cash (who, by the way, is totally ignoring me), runs the very tip of her French-manicured nail down the length of his arm (I guess so that I can see in a fully up-close-and-personal kind of way, how she now has an all-access pass to the body of the boy we once only dreamed about), and goes, "Awesome. Everything's perfect."

And I just sit there, holding my smile 'til the corners of my mouth begin to twitch.

I wish I could honestly say that none of that bothers me. That seeing her sitting in that bucket seat as though it were her rightful throne, casually fondling Cash Davis's extremities simply because she can, doesn't bug me in the least. That knowing she's probably going further with him than she ever did with her cousin is of no concern to me. That getting a front row center seat to today's performance of "sit back and watch while I demonstrate just how perfectly, and easily, I succeeded at everything *we* set out to do, and how you *didn't*," is truly no biggie.

But that would be a lie.

Because the awful truth is that no matter how phony I think Sloane's become, no matter how mean and shallow I know Cash to be, the truth is Sloane has easily succeeded where I failed. She's claimed what I once wanted. And now she's sitting before me, like a tiny, perfect, blond goddess next to her sexy, hunky, verbally challenged prince.

While I take a backseat, as alone and unimpressive as ever.

But it's not like I share any of that with her. Instead I just force myself to look her in the eye, and smile even bigger. And then I gaze around the inside of the Hummer, thinking how it's actually quite a bit smaller than I would've guessed.

"So where should we drop you?" she asks, her eyes traveling over my outfit, starting at my scruffy black Target ballet flats, working up the super-narrow inseam of my straight from SoHo, stovepipe jeans, and ultimately coming to rest on my black "I Wanna Be Sedated" Ramone's T-shirt that Easton accidentally left behind but said I could wear until he needed it again. "Home?"

Originally I was headed home. But that was before she appeared. So now, everything's changed. I mean, let's not forget the most important detail here—the fact that I'm riding in a *Hummer*. An object my mom finds so despicable, has such tremendous disdain for, and holds personally responsible for some of the planet's most egregious disasters (as in, global warming, dependence on foreign oil, parking space hogging), that I'll be damned if I'll waste this once in a lifetime, tailor-made, perfect opportunity to totally freak her out.

So I go, "If you guys could just drop me off right outside the café, then that would be great." Then I look straight into Sloane's blue contact enhanced eyes and smile my heart out, as though this is all so totally and completely pleasant, and that there's no hard feelings or anything at all awkward, weird, or forced about any of this.

Cash pulls into the empty space directly in front of the café, and I watch as my mom stops clearing a table so she can scowl at the big black beast, her face containing all the disdain and contempt I'd hoped for. So of course I take my time climbing out of the back, grabbing my backpack, and trying to milk this moment for all that it's worth. And after waving good-bye I turn toward the window, laughing when I see my mom's jaw dropped down around her knees.

And just as I'm about to go inside and fend off all the expected inquiries, Sloane sticks her head out the window and goes, "Hey, Winter, I almost forgot to tell you. I saw your dad last night on TV. *So cool!* Tell him I said hi, k?" Then she smiles and waves, as Cash backs onto the street, and now I know why they gave me a ride.

December, only X amount of shopping days left, people! 2006

11:10 P.M.

Current Mood—Cautiously hopeful

Current Music—"It's My Life"—original 80's version

Quote of the Day—"The fish dies because he opens his mouth."

—Spanish proverb

Sometimes You Can't Make It On Your Own

This just in: PRINCESS PINK SACKED BY CAPTAIN WORLD—PASTEL POSSE SE-CRETLY CELEBRATES.

It's official. Princess Pink is back on the block. Though sadly for her she didn't realize it until it was too late. Until she was already on-stage, all dressed up in a bedsheet working overtime as a toga, hop-ing for the highest bid on the much anticipated "Slave Day." (Yes, you read that correctly, and even though that's not the real name as I can't exactly reveal that due to issues of privacy and anonymity, trust me that it's basically the same exact gist. Amounting to yet an-other misguided, politically incorrect, completely insensitive, school-sponsored activity that will do nothing to benefit moi, but everything to support the junior senior promgoers). While Captain World, who clearly was expected to dip into the deep pockets of his never-ending trust fund so that he could "purchase" the cow he'd presumably already "milked" for free, completely no-showed due to an assumed lack of interest. Spiteful, jealous posse members were overheard squealing with glee as they watched Princess Pink sell for the humiliatingly low price of twelve dollars and ninety-five cents, to an overexcited, presumably horny, pimple-faced freshman who apparently reads the same bathroom walls as me.

And just moments after the festivities ended, yours truly (Eleanor) headed to her much dreaded gym class, unobtrusively trailing behind Pastel Posse members and listening in as they said:

"Omigod! Did you see her?"

"Omigod! So sad!"

"Kind of an ego bust, but whatever."

"Not like she didn't deserve it."

"You could totally see through that sheet."

"Stupid skank."

"Fucking bitch."

And as they veered down another hall, I continued toward the gym, all the while shaking my head and thinking, *And those are her friends?*

And as unbelievable as this may sound, I kind of feel sorry for her. So in honor of that, today there will be no list.

Adios,

Eleanor Rigby

Twenty-three

Just three days before the much dreaded (well, at least by me) school talent show, Rey corners me. Which, when you consider how he works for my mom, sits next to me in Chemistry, and is now fully aware of how I'm back to eating lunch in the library, kind of makes me wonder why he waited so long in the first place. But I guess after his failed attempt at sending Hayden in to convince me to come back out and rejoin the table, he pretty much gave up.

And believe me, I know for a fact that he's the one who sent her, because it didn't take all that long to get her to confess.

"He feels really bad about the whole thing," she said, taking the chair across from mine and eyeing my sandwich.

"So you know?" I asked, quickly averting my eyes and feeling all weird and embarrassed yet also a little curious about what she actually thought of all this.

But she just shrugged. "Believe me, *everyone* knows. But I still think you should just relax already. I mean, move on and get over it. There's tons of guys out there. And once you finally realize that, I'm sure you'll be able to just get on with your life and forget it ever happened. It's like, what's the big deal? It was just a kiss, right?"

But hearing her say that made me realize how she didn't really understand anything. "Hayden," I finally said, lifting my head to look at her. "When you *really* like the guy, it's *never* just a kiss."

And the moment it was out there, spoken like a fact, I suddenly felt a lot better. I mean, it's not like I was the first girl to pine after a guy who preferred someone else, so there was a pretty good chance that I wouldn't be the last.

But Hayden just looked at me, nodding slowly, and running her fingers against the smooth, fake wood desk. "So, do you mind if I join you in here sometimes?" she asked. "Because I get kind of sick of hanging around the guys all the time, you know?"

And I just looked at her and smiled, feeling relieved that I wouldn't always have to be alone.

But now, just as I'm reaching for the beaker I need so I can fill it with, um, *stuff* (okay, so I don't really know the difference between a proton, a neutron, and an electron, and have absolutely no idea what the heck I'm supposed to be doing with this beaker. I mean, just because I'm in honors English doesn't mean I know anything about science), Rey grabs my wrist and goes, "Winter, we need to talk."

And without even looking at him I just pull my hand away and go, "Okay, but I need to finish this first." And I say that with such authority, like there is nothing more important to me than bringing this experiment to its ultimate and final conclusion (whatever that may be). And then I turn away, knowing that I need to start moving at a slowed-down pace, and just take my time with the measuring, charting, and checking everything thrice, doing whatever it takes to ensure I don't fin- ish until long after the bell rings, if even then.

But Rey's not having any of it. Shaking his head in frustra- tion he goes, "Winter, *please.*"

And the way he sounds when he says that, so full of an- guish and desperation, makes me drop the beaker, halt the ex- periment, and finally look up at him.

"Okay," he says quietly, gazing at me intently. "I'm not sure how to say this, but I really feel like I need to apologize for what happened. It was impulsive and stupid, and I never meant to embarrass you or make you feel so uncomfortable around me." He presses his lips together and looks away. "And you've got to believe me when I say that if I could do anything to erase it, I would. Because now I can see what a huge mistake it was. But since there's no way I can go back and undo it, I was hop- ing that maybe you'd consider coming back to the lunch table, so that we can move forward and hopefully just be friends again. What do you say?"

He's looking at me, searching my face, and I know that he's actually being really sincere, trying really hard to convince me of just how much he means all this.

But what he doesn't understand is how despite his an- guished, heartfelt, sincerely crafted apology, he's actually made me feel even worse. Because from my side of the table, all I can hear are the echo of words like *sorry, stupid, impulsive, uncomfortable, huge mistake, erase . . .* And believe me, the pleading look on his face, and his desperate attempt to renew our friendship, really can't compete when it goes head-to-head with all that.

But it's not like I'm about to share any of that with him, so instead, I just nod and smile, and maybe even mutter some- thing sounding vaguely like, "Okay." And then I force myself to focus my attention solely on this completely confusing ex- periment, filling beakers, and logging data, like it's just another day in chem class, and that my eyes aren't really stinging, and that there's no huge lump crowding my throat.

Now that Sloane and Cash are history (and no, I still don't know why, but I'm working on it), she's totally back to being tight with the Pastel Posse. Seriously, it's like every time I see her, she's completely surrounded by them, as they hover all around her, offering up phony solace and insincere support, like a newly installed airbag in a factory-controlled crash.

And for someone who was just recently entrenched in her second round of friendlessness, now thanks to my dad, his new show, and his sixteenth minute of fame, all these kids, most of whom I don't even know, are waving at me in the hall, smiling politely in class, and pretty much doing whatever it takes to get my attention in a friendly, polite, nonthreatening way. I mean, it's like virtually overnight I've managed to graduate from being someone who goes completely unnoticed, to a definite person of interest.

Which would be totally cool and all, if it actually had anything to do with me.

And now, the day I've been dreading for weeks is finally here. The one where I had to choose between faking sick—where I'd get to stay home, tucked safely in bed, far away from school and everyone who goes there (yet also suffering through my mom's foul-tasting, highly suspicious, homeopathic medicine cures)—or sucking it up and grabbing a front row center seat for the stupid, freaking high-school talent show that I definitely don't want to see. I mean, really, "Ocean Idols?" Who are they kidding? Yet, knowing full well that the dreaded administrations of Dr. Mom are definitely the bigger evil, I chose school.

So I'm climbing the auditorium steps, searching for an empty seat, when Sloane, Jaci, Holly, and Claire start waving their hands all around, like they actually want me to join them or something.

But I know better, so I just ignore them. Because even though they've been making twice the effort to be nice to me lately (well, at least *their* version of nice), I'm still not entirely convinced that they actually want me to sit with them, in a public place, in front of all of their adoring fans.

So when I see Hayden, Evan, Elijah, and Clark, who are also waving at me, I start heading toward them. Because even though I hang with Hayden sometimes, I still kind of miss hanging with the guys. And with Rey safely stowed away backstage, preparing for his big debut, the coast is pretty much clear.

And just as I get to their row, and am inching toward an empty seat, Sloane stands up, cups her hands around her mouth, and over the din of the completely packed auditorium yells, "Hey, Winter! What the hell are you doing? Get over here already! We saved you a freaking seat!"

And just like that, everyone's staring at me.

Including Hayden, Evan, Elijah, and Clark, who are staring with a really strange, will-she-or-won't-she look on their faces.

I stand there, caught between two worlds (literally!), knowing that I now have to choose between some extremely popular girls who have gone out of their way to be mean and nasty and totally horrible to me, and my loyal friends who've been nothing but nice, accepting, and supportive, and who I've really missed hanging out with.

Then I take a deep breath and make the only choice that I can. And as I wave at Hayden, her eyes go all stiff and wide in an oh-no-she-did-not kind of way, then I head for the empty seat between Sloane, Jaci, Holly, and Claire. Reminding myself the entire way just how great this will be for the blog. Which is definitely, completely, and absolutely the only reason why I'm even doing this.

"Hey," I say, crossing my legs just like them, making a conscious effort to mirror their body language, which accord-

ing to one of the self-help books I read last summer is the
quickest, nonverbal way to establish a sense of belonging and
camaraderie.

"Hey," they say, all together now, scrutinizing my entire
outfit, and smiling in a way that could never, under any circumstances, be considered sincere.

And then Sloane looks at me, eyes all wide, and goes,
"Omigod, this so reminds me. Remember 'Lady Marmalade'?"

And when I look at her, I can't help but think how amazing
it is that now that she's officially the sophomore class It girl, it
took one of my dad's headshots to appear in *People* magazine's
"Comeback!" issue to green-light her admission that *yes, at one
time in the not-so-distant past, we actually were kind of good friends.*
But I don't say that. In fact, I don't really say anything. I just
smile and nod and wait for what's next.

Then she looks at Jaci, Holly, and Claire and goes, "Omigod,
major scandal! Major!" Then she rolls her eyes, and shakes her
head, like her whole entire life has just been way too full and
far too glamorous to keep it all straight. "Details later." She
smiles.

And even though I don't really do anything other than
nod, I'm actually wondering if one of those "details" might be
how in the midst of all of her "bad girl scandal-making" I had
to stop and explain just exactly why we were getting hauled
into the principal's office. Since that whole entire time she had
no idea what the lyrics even meant.

And just as I'm thinking how I might just go ahead and
share that, the lights are suddenly dimmed and Principal
Meyer takes the stage, grabs the mike, and introduces the first
act, which unfortunately consists of four ambitious freshmen,
dressed all Fergie-style, while performing a not-so-family-
friendly dance routine to "My Humps." Which, by the way, is
not only ten times worse than my own talent show debacle, but
also way more embarrassing than it sounds.

And after somehow surviving *that,* some girl I've never

talked to but who sits like two rows behind me in geometry, walks onstage, situates herself at this creaky, old, donated piano, and starts belting out a shaky, warbled version of that song "Fallin'" that leaves me cringing.

Although to be honest, I'm mostly cringing at the things Sloane and her friends are saying, as they hurl insults so mean, so cruel, so heartless, and so degrading, even Simon Cowell would blush.

And then somewhere after like eight more totally excruciating, completely embarrassing acts, Principal Meyer comes back on stage and announces, "And now, ladies and gentlemen, I present to you Ocean High's very own Social Exile!"

And then the curtain opens again, and I see Pete on drums, Mick on guitar, and standing smack-dab in the center of the stage is Rey, with his guitar strapped to his long, lean torso and his longish dark hair hanging in his eyes. And as he grabs the mike and gets ready to sing, my eyes search the stage for Shay, who, I heard via Hayden, is back to singing backup.

Only she's not there.

And just as I'm thinking how odd that is, and wondering if maybe she couldn't get time off from school or something, Rey goes, "This one goes out to—well, you know who you are."

And then right before he starts singing, Jaci looks at us, her eyes all wide as she goes, "Omigod, does he really go here? Because he is *so über-hot!*"

And then Holly goes, "Omigod, *sexy!* And those jeans aren't even designer!"

And then Claire starts to say something at the same exact time the band starts playing, so Sloane looks over, makes an angry face, and goes, "Shhh!"

And me? Well, I just sit there as solid and immobile as a block of kitchen-counter granite as I listen to Social Exile play the opening strains to their awesome version of "A Hazy Shade of Winter," while wondering if Rey really is looking right at me as he sings, or if I'm just so freaked-out and panicked that I'm somehow imagining it.

And when the song is finally, mercifully over, Sloane, who's been rotating her head back and forth between the stage and me that entire time like she's spotting a tennis match, grabs my arm and goes, "Omigod! That was for *you!*"

And then Principal Meyer comes back on, and once he's quieted down all the hooting and clapping and cries for an encore, he says, "Folks, I'm sorry to have to say this, but it's just been brought to my attention that only one member of Social Exile is actually enrolled here at Ocean High, so I'm afraid they will have to be disqualified."

Within seconds the entire auditorium erupts in screams, shouts, boos, and flying objects, and deciding to take full advantage of all the chaos, I peel Sloane's fingers off my arm, grab my purse, dodge through outraged, rioting students, and get the hell out of there.

And the second I'm outside, I remember how today is the last day before Winter Break.

Which means it's a short day.

Which means I run off campus and all the way home.

December, dangerously close to Xmas 2006

9:45 A.M.

Current Mood—Fraught

Current Music—The "all sad songs all the time" station that broad-casts only in my head

Quote of the Day—"When you come to a fork in the road, take it."
—Yogi Berra

I'm Only Happy When It Rains

Number of times Princess Pink has called and left a voice message: 5

Number of times Princess Pink has left a text message: 3

1. OMG Call if u wan2 go xmas shopg
2. Coffee Strbks L8R
3. Call me 2nt at 7

Number of times I acknowledge and/or returned any of these messages: 0

Number of times I've left my room: 3 (but only to use the bathroom, as I've got a drawerful of junk food to rival any White House bunker and so probably won't need to vacate the premises until I diminish all supplies which, by my calculations, will not occur until approximately sometime around the day after New Year's).

Number of times my mother has stood in my doorway shaking her head and going, "For the last time, what is going on with you?": 2 many 2 count.

So here's **The List**, but only 'cause you got so mad when I omitted it last time.

20. After much sleuthing, Old Eleanor finally got to the bottom of P. P. and Captain World's breakup. And the truth is, they didn't break up. At least, not at first. You see, rumor has it that at the exact moment the "slave auction" began, El Capitan suffered the sudden onset of a severe case of abdominal distress, cafeteria worker's revenge, or food poisoning, whatever you want to call it. Apparently things got so bad so quickly, he was left with no choice but to vacate the premises and rush home, leaving no time to contact P. P. and give her the heads-up. So P. P., unaware of anything other than the fact that she was stuck onstage, all alone, with no boyfriend bidder in sight, unfortunately allowed her old friend, Insecurity, to take over as she assumed she'd been ditched. So, hell-bent on revenge after suffering such humiliation, she paid off the freshman (tossed him a crisp twenty and called it even), and wasted no time in hooking up with Captain World's newly single best friend (who will be referred to from here on as "Last Name"). When P. P. finally got around to listening to the Captain's hugely apologetic, albeit tardy, cell phone message, it was too late—the damage (not to mention the "deed") was done, and Last Name was in the shower, ridding himself of the evidence. And though it's safe to say that P. P. does *not* place much (if any) value on her friendships or their corresponding commitments, Last Name, apparently, does. As rumor has it that he either (*a*) felt so badly about the betrayal he needed to confess his sins and beg forgiveness, or (more likely), (*b*) he felt obligated to inform his friend of his girlfriend's skanky ways. Whatever the motive, the fact remains that, using his bathroom line, he placed a call to Captain World, filling him in on all the sordid details, while failing to men-

Kiss & Blog

189

tion any of this to P. P., who was slinking out of his house at the exact moment Captain World pulled into the drive to confront her.

And that's when they broke up.

Over and out,

Eleanor Rigby

Twenty-four

Talk about a social exile. By my fifth day of hanging in my room refusing to come out, my mom barges in, and believe me, from the look on her face, it's clear she means business.

"Okay, so what the heck is going on? It's been almost a week, and I'm through playing games with you. I know you're going through a rough time, and I've done my best to try and make things easier for you, but, Winter, I'm just about at the end of my rope here," she says, plopping herself hard on the edge of my bed and gazing at me with so much worry, despair, and concern, it makes me feel completely guilty and awful.

But that doesn't mean that I tell her.

"I'm fine, seriously," I say, trying to look as though I really do mean it by sitting up straighter, and running my hands through my tangled, messy, greasy hair.

"Listen, Dave, Autumn, and I are heading out to the Winter Fantasy Art Festival. And I know how much you always enjoy that. So how about you take a quick shower, get dressed, and come along with us, and then we'll grab dinner somewhere later."

But even though she thinks I "always enjoy that," I'm sorry to say that these days enjoyment falls pretty low on my list of priorities. It's somewhere down there with sunshine, showers, and smiling. So I just look at her and shake my head. I mean, I feel bad about being such a big disappointment, and I feel even worse knowing how bad I'm making her feel, but that doesn't mean I'm willing to budge. "No, thanks." I stretch, making a big show of lifting my arms high above my head. "I think I'm just gonna take a hot shower, and then maybe head outside and take a walk," I say, filling her with false hope, while knowing full well how there's no way I'm doing any of those things.

But she just looks at me, staring at me for so long I squirm. Then finally she sighs, hoists herself off my bed, and heads for the door. And then almost as an afterthought, she turns and goes, "So, maybe during your walk, you can head on over to the café and fill in for Rey."

"Rey's not coming in today?" I ask, immediately wondering why, since he's got like the best work ethic of anyone I know, and has never been late, never gets sick, and wouldn't even contemplate pulling a no-show.

But she just shrugs and goes, "Can you cover for him?"

Do I *want* to cover for him? Not exactly. But I no longer feel I have much of a choice. So I just nod, climb out of bed, and for the first time in a long time, head for the shower.

Okay, so here's the deal. I know you probably think that all this high drama, fainting lady stuff is all about the talent show and that surprising song dedication and my pathetic inability to finally get real with the guy I've been not so secretly in love with this whole entire time, right?

Well, yeah. But that's only part of it. The other part is that my whole life feels like it's just seconds away from completely imploding, right before my very eyes, and I don't know what, or even *if*, I should do anything to stop it.

And even though I know this probably sounds completely crazy, I still have to say that it's almost like I can trace all of this crazy chaos right back to the very second when I blew out those sixteen sinking birthday pie candles. And how immediately afterward I feared I hadn't been quite specific enough.

And believe me, I'm not making this up, because if you'll just follow along and review all the evidence with me, I think you'll begin to see how it's all starting to come true:

1. Rey and Shay. Shay is out of the band and out of Rey's life. Or at least that's what Hayden wrote in an e-mail she sent and that I've still yet to answer.

2. Sloane. Sloane is making no attempt to curb her incessant, insane, insistent efforts to reach me. And as far as I'm concerned that pretty much covers the "Sloane" part of the wish. Even though, quite frankly, I was actually thinking more in terms of revenge than reunion, but then again, I forgot to be specific, so this is what I got.

3. The Talent Show. Well, what I really wanted was to get out of performing in it, and obviously I did. Though I think we can all see how that turned out.

4. Mom. Okay, that was just sort of a general wish, as in "I want her to be happy and healthy, but maybe shave her legs once in a while, and perhaps learn to let me be when I want to be let be and hug me when I want to be hugged (which really isn't as of-

ten as she thinks).” And so far, I admit, there doesn't seem to be any major consequences to that, but that still doesn't mean I can relax.

5. Blog. The blog. Well, that's the most unbelievable part of all.

Just the other day when I ran home from school, straight from the talent show fiasco and into my room, I tossed my purse on my bed and headed straight for my computer, where I signed into my blog, feeling this desperate need to connect with this anonymous group of people, who happen to read all this stuff about my life, and therefore think they know me. I mean, at that moment, the urge to make contact felt so powerful, so overwhelming, and so all-consuming, that I was like a junkie craving a fix.

So I started typing, fast, furious, crazy-lady typing. I mean, it was as though my fingers just couldn't hit those keys quick enough. And I was spilling all kinds of secrets, Sloane's secrets, my secrets, seriously, I was just venting about all this stuff, like how Rey sang for me, and how Sloane's acting all nice to me because my dad's on TV, and how I really, really miss hanging at the lunch table with Hayden, Evan, Elijah, and Clark. And I was using real names, and writing about real scenarios, but when it came time to post, I suddenly realized how I couldn't use a single word of it. Because absolutely none of it was in code. And left like that, without some major editing, it was just way too revealing, and would totally compromise my anonymity.

But even while I was deleting it, I was still feeling that same, lonely need to connect. So I pacified myself by reading through all of my latest comments, until I finally came across one from some guy claiming to be an agent, and who wrote something about how he was interested in developing my blog into a book.

Well, obviously, it didn't take long for me to realize that it was a total scam. So I just scrolled right past it and moved on to the next comment.

But still, even after I'd finished reading through all of them, there was something about that fake agent message that kept nagging at me. So, against my better judgment, I scrolled back up to reread it.

Then I wrote down his name and went Google-fishing.

And I spent the next two hours studying every single relevant hit that I could possibly find.

As I continued to research, I started to realize that this guy was entirely legit. Because from what I'd read, he really was a literary agent, and really had handled quite a few other blog-to-book deals, including some stuff I'd actually seen and/or heard of. And I started to get really, really excited when I realized how I was quite possibly being offered the opportunity of a lifetime.

Yet I also knew I had no choice but to decline.

I mean, I think we can all agree that yes, Sloane has been and probably will continue to be a total bitch. And that I, for one, have suffered greatly at the claws of her French-manicured hands. And even though this offer should have everything to do with *me,* and nothing to do with *her,* I still can't get comfortable with the idea of exposing her like that. And it's not because I'd actually fallen for her stupid, phony, pseudo-friendship attempts, because believe me, that stuff was as blatantly transparent as ever.

It was more the fact of how very recently I've come to the conclusion of just how wrong it is to divulge other people's secrets. Never mind sell them. I mean, honestly, when someone tells you a secret, they really are expecting you to keep it. And even though I might have betrayed that confidence by blurting them out in my blog, the fact is, I did everything I could not to reveal just exactly who those secrets belong to, and yet all of them were still 100 percent true. And since pretty much everyone knows how intrusive and in your business the whole publishing world is, I knew that if I accepted a deal like that then I'd totally risk outing Sloane. And really, as mad and betrayed as I am, when it comes right down to it, I just don't know if I have the stomach for it.

I mean, originally, all I was after was some good old-fashioned revenge. But now it's all starting to feel so heavy, like such a growing burden, that I'm just not sure how much longer I can keep at it.

And that's when I took to my bed. Where I spent the next several days agonizing over the mess I'd made, and wondering what, if anything, I should do about it.

The second I walk in the café I know my mom has completely played me.

"Hey," I say, heading into the back room to grab an apron, as Rey stops cleaning the counter in mid-wipe just so he can stand there and stare at me in a way that tells me he definitely isn't in on this game.

"What're you doing here?" he asks, dropping the sponge and following me.

"My mom asked me to come in and help cover today," I say, reaching back to tie my apron, unwilling to tell him the truth of what she *actually* said, and how she totally tricked me into coming here.

"Well, you can bail if you want. Everything's under control," he says, shrugging and looking pretty uncomfortable to be all alone in a room with me.

But I just shake my head and grab a rubber band out of the desk drawer, so that I can pull my hair back into a tight, neat, food server's ponytail.

And just as I'm smoothing the wispy parts back, the bell on the front door rings. And I'm just about to say, "I got it," at the exact same moment I hear Sloane's voice go, "No, her mom doesn't just work here, she totally owns this place. Duh."

And then I look at Rey with my eyes all panicked and wide. But he just shakes his head, and in a calm, sure voice says, "No worries." Then he heads out front, while I hover by the door so that I can hide and eavesdrop simultaneously.

"I usually get that Purple Berry thingy," I hear Jaci say, tacking her adorable giggle onto the end of that.

"Whatever. Um, what's the My Cherry Amore?" Sloane asks, in her cutest little-girl voice.

And I just stand there listening as Rey recites the long list of healthy, wholesome, organic ingredients that can be found in my mom's newest cherry smoothie creation, until Sloane finally cuts him off somewhere in the middle and goes, "Okay, you talked me into it."

So then of course the rest of them all order it, too, including Jaci, who apparently bears no loyalty to her "usual" now that Sloane's in charge. And as Rey is probably busy making them (and I say "probably" since as I can't actually see him, I'm pretty much forced to rely on my imagination here), Sloane says in her flirtiest voice, "Omigod, you're that lead singer of, oh, I forget, what's the name of your band?"

And then Rey mumbles, "Social Exile."

And Sloane goes, "Yeah, that's it. Social Exile." Like he needs her to confirm it.

And then she pauses, which in my imagination means that she's leaning on the counter, flashing maximum, Miracle Bra–enhanced cleavage while gazing at Rey, and trying to think of something else to say. And when she finally decides, she goes, "You guys were *sooo* amazing. I never even heard that song before, but you totally deserved to win. I can't believe how lame Principal Meyer is, what a dickwad."

And then Rey mumbles, "Um, thanks."

And then the phone rings.

And since they don't know that I'm hiding back here, and since I can't under any circumstances blow my cover and risk having them hear my voice, I just stand there, counting the rings, until Rey finally goes, "Uh, just a sec. I'll be right back."

And as he runs off to get the phone I hear Jaci say, "Omigod, *what* are you doing? You're totally flirting with him and I thought you said he liked Winter?"

Then Sloane goes, "Please. How could he like her? She's a fat loser."

And even though Sloane has done nothing to make me think she'd say anything other than that, still, I have to admit that hearing her actually say that out loud hurts so bad I can hardly believe it.

I slump down to the floor, dropping my head in my hands, as my eyes swell with tears, as I hear Jaci say, "Well, for someone who's supposedly such a fat loser you sure call her a lot."

And then Holly goes, "Yeah, I mean, what's up with that?"

And then Sloane goes, "Uh, hello? Her dad's like totally famous again. Not to mention how they're filming some family episodes next season. And believe me, I plan to be right there when the cameras start rolling, because no way is she getting all the attention. She's like, a no-talent dork with a really bad TV personality. Trust me, she'll thank me when she realizes she's too big of a social retard to handle the spotlight."

And even though part of me feels even worse when I hear her say that, the other part is thinking, *What family episode? And how does she even know this stuff? I mean, even I didn't know about that.*

"Listen, Rey is totally smoking hot," she continues. "And it's just a matter of time 'til he's mine. It's not my fault if he doesn't know it yet."

And then they all start laughing. Because, well, obviously you can see how hilarious that is.

And then, apparently all pumped up on princess power and an overwhelming sense of her own importance, Sloane goes,

"Listen, Winter's a zero, a nobody. So it's not like he'll even miss her."

Then Claire whispers, "You guys, shhh! He's totally coming back!"

And as Rey continues making their smoothies, I wipe my face, raise my butt off the floor, grab my purse, and run out the back door, where I go home and write.

To: Calvin Burke
From: Eleanor Rigby
Subject: Your offer

Dear Mr. Burke,
Thank you for your interest in my blog, as well as your offer of representation. I'm very interested in hearing more about your thoughts and ideas, and just what kind of project you have in mind. Hardcover? Paperback? Podcast?
Please feel free to contact me at your earliest convenience.

Sincerely,
Eleanor Rigby

Twenty-five

It's been two days. Two days since my mom tricked me into seeing Rey. Two days since Sloane revealed herself to be an even worse person than even I could have imagined. Two days since my dad called and asked if I'd, "Please just take a day or two to think about making a brief appearance in *ACT II,* season two, before you say no and hang up without giving it any real thought." Two days since Rey left a message, seconds after discovering I'd fled out the back door, and asked (almost in a begging kind of way) for me to *please* call him back. Two days since I e-mailed that Calvin Burke guy who's yet to e-mail me back.

Which also means it's Christmas.

"Oh, Winter, thank you!" Autumn says, getting up to hug me, and looking truly psyched about the art book and the new set of acrylic paints I bought her the day before yesterday.

I trace my finger over the shiny glass beads on the bracelet she made (that matches the necklace she crafted for my birthday), then I smile at my mom who really outdid herself this year by giving both Autumn and me our very own laptops.

"I thought you might be sick of sharing that tired old secondhand computer." She shrugged, her eyes showing just how pleased she is that we're happy.

And then while we're busy polishing off the remaining bits of our family's version of a traditional Christmas breakfast, consisting of free-range egg white omelets, tofu scramble, organic strawberries, whole grain muffins, and two pots of shade-grown coffee, my mom looks at us both and drops a bomb. "Winter, Autumn," she says, eyes fixed and unwavering. "I want you both to know that I'm planning to close the café for several weeks for renovations." She takes a sip of her coffee and watches us carefully.

Autumn and I both stare at her, our eyes wide. "Are you serious?" we ask.

She takes a sip of fresh-squeezed, organic, heavy-on-the-pulp orange juice, and nods. "Dave has already drawn up the plans. We're taking over the space next door, so I can expand the number of tables and still have enough room for a small stage for readings, and concerts and such. And if everything goes as planned, we should start knocking down walls the day after New Year's."

"But, how different is it going to be?" I ask, feeling kind of put off by all this. I mean, my mom's always been kind of stuck in the seventies, not to mention stuck in her ideas. And words like *makeover* and *renovation* have never been part of her every-day vocabulary (unless of course she's talking about the government). But looking at her now, I mean really looking at her, I suddenly realize that things have been changing for quite some time, only I've been too self-absorbed and wrapped up in my own dramas to really stop and take notice.

But now I can see how her lips are shining with something that looks a little more substantial than her usual, haphazard swipe of Burt's Bees Balm, and how she no longer smells like a freshly squeezed batch of patchouli oil, but instead of something lighter, more floral, with just the tiniest hint of citrus. And if I'm not mistaken, she might even have added a little product to her hair, because now that I'm looking at it, I can see how her curls are much softer, and way more defined and separated (as opposed to her usual spray of frizz). I mean, don't get me wrong, she's still my granola-chomping, tree-hugging, hairy-legged mom. She's just a better groomed, slightly renovated version.

And then I wonder if it's because of Dave. I mean, it's like she and Autumn and Dave have become this little family unit, going to the Winter Art Festival, attending First Thursday Art Walk, heck, they even took a trip to L.A. to check out the new Getty Villa Museum. And where was I while all of this family bonding was taking place? I was hunkered down in my room, bed curtain drawn, doing my very best to avoid any and all human contact.

"So, because New Year's is all about saying good-bye to the old and ringing in the new, I thought we'd start clearing out the space a little early, and just throw ourselves a big old party! Just a big huge bash where we can move away from the past and just really revel in the coming new year, what do you think?" She looks at us excitedly.

Um, since when does she use words like revel *and* bash*? And when did she look forward to "moving away from the past"? I mean, she's usually hanging on to the past with both hands, and it's like a brutal game of tug-of-war to get her to let go!* But I don't say any of that. Instead, I just go, "Um, sounds okay, I guess." And even though I'm fully aware of how it actually sounds far better than just "okay," this is a whole lot of change in a short period of time, and it's going to take a little longer than five minutes for me to adjust.

But as always, the ever excited, open-to-everything Autumn just starts jumping up and down in her seat, with her usual uninhibited display of energy. "Cool! Can I invite everyone?" she asks hopefully.

And when I look at her, I realize how she means just exactly that. Like she truly believes that everyone in her whole freaking school, staff members and custodians included, is her friend.

So, of course, my mom goes, "Invite anyone you want! The more the merrier! In fact, I forgot to mention this, but Rey and his band have agreed to provide the entertainment. Which, by the way, I hear you're very much missed on backup these days, young lady," she says, winking at me and smiling.

Um, since when does my mom wink? Or make any kind of cutesy facial expressions for that matter?

And then suddenly I realize—this is the *Mom* part of the birthday wish. And even though I'd originally only hoped for a slightly modified version, once again, my lack of specificity lead me to this—a complete and total overhaul!

And just as I'm about to mumble the same lame excuse for the totally valid and completely logical reason as to why I've been an absentee backup singer, the doorbell rings.

And as my mom gets up to answer it, Autumn and I decide to split the last muffin.

Then just as I pop a big ol' piece into my mouth, I hear my mom go, "Oh, Dave!"

And when she comes back into the room, she's wearing a beautiful conflict-free diamond engagement ring.

December 29, 2006

7:45 P.M.

Current Mood—Used and abused

Current Music—Out-of-tune high-pitched yips from the little Maltese dog next door

Quote of the Day—"Have no friends not equal to yourself."—Confucius

204

Sugar, We're Going Down

Yesterday I finally answered Princess Pink's urgent 911 call and allowed her to invite herself to my party. And then, just to keep up the appearance of friendship that never, ever faltered, just to banish any lingering suspicion I might have had about the sketchy intentions behind her sudden renewed interest in me—she told me a secret. Can you even believe it? So I guess it's safe to assume that's she's not exactly a reader of this blog.

But I know the real reason she wants to come. And believe me, it has nothing to do with her getting suddenly sentimental and singing our made-up (slightly dirty) lyrics to "Auld Lang Syne" that we co-wrote in the seventh grade. Nope, the reason she wants to come is because Gift Bag will be there. Remember him? The one I so recklessly, foolishly gave away all those months ago? Well, now, apparently, Princess Pink plans to come to my party so that she can walk away with her very own Gift Bag. And hey, who am I to stop her from trying?

And so, The List:

21. Rumor has it that P. P. exacted revenge on Last Name when she called his ex (who it turns out was not really his ex as

they were merely "on a break") and sent her a photo of his retreating bare ass, captured on her camera phone as he headed for the shower. When Ex, who not only considered herself *not* single (she was *sure* they could work it out), but also as a sort of mentor to P. P., received the photo, she went absolutely, totally, and completely berserk. Chaos ensued, breakups occurred, recriminations were yelled, and all the cheerleaders from frosh/soph to varsity were completely divided. But as the holidays approached tempers softened, anger eased, and both original couples decided to forgive and forget as they tentatively, yet happily, reunited. With P. P. staying with Captain World just long enough to unwrap his (much hinted for) present, before dumping him via e-mail sometime during the early morning hours of December 26.

Good tidings to you, too!

Eleanor Rigby

Twenty-six

By Friday when I still haven't heard from Mr. Calvin Burke, agent to the most glittering of literati, I'm so over myself, so sick of obsessively checking my e-mail, and rereading his original message over and over again, searching for hidden meanings in his words and punctuation choices, and wondering if it's all been some kind of mistake, hoax, or even worse, just a foolish, impulsive offer that he now sincerely regrets ever making, that I begin to wonder if maybe, perhaps, *I* should be the one changing my mind.

I mean, obviously I'd chosen to move forward in a major fit of rage and vengeance. And I think we all know how you pretty much can't find a worse time to make a life-defining decision. And even though it's obvious that Sloane is a self-serving brat, and probably deserves to be exposed for the awful person that she truly is, there's still this growing part of me that's more than a little freaked by all this, because let's face it, exposing Sloane also means exposing *me*.

And who's to say she won't retaliate and tell a few of my own secrets?

So with my head feeling all foggy and bloated with the weight of all that, I decide to head over to the café and hang out for a while. I mean, I hadn't been there since the day I heard Sloane plotting a hostile takeover on my number one crush (well, actually number two, right after Joaquin Phoenix). And as my mom has been so busy lately, with all the packing and moving and just trying to get everything ready for the big renovation and party, I figure the least I can do is show up, make some small talk, and maybe even pitch in and help.

But when I walk inside, I hardly recognize the place. Because even though it's barely been a week, the whole entire space has been completely transformed. I mean, the floors have been stripped down to their final layer of concrete, and now with all the fixtures and furnishings gone, but with the antique chandeliers still hanging, it actually looks pretty cool. Kind of industrial chic, and not at all shabby like you might think. And since the walls have been stripped completely bare of all of their formerly down-home, shrine signage to dorky songs from the seventies, they're now serving as these huge floor-to-ceiling canvases that are completely covered in a riot of color, making for the most amazing, continuous, wall-to-wall mural, that based on a limited amount of knowledge salvaged from long-ago childhood art classes, seems to be telling an epic tale of life, beauty, truth, creation, celebration, and rebirth.

And as I stand there gazing at it, trying to soak it all up and take it all in, the person who seems most likely to be responsible for all of this approaches me with a wet paintbrush that's dripping a trail of cobalt blue, and inadvertently turning the concrete floor into a Jackson Pollock canvas.

"Hey," I say, gazing from him to the still wet walls. "Is my mom around?"

But skinny smoker dude just shakes his head, and then nods toward the wall before us. "So? What do you think?" he asks, looking at me with his head cocked to the side, like he just might actually consider my completely amateur, perhaps even bogus, opinion.

I gaze at the swirls of color so vibrant they almost seem to be pulsating, then I look at him and go, "I don't even know the right words. It's completely amazing. But it's more than that." I stop and stare at the walls and shrug. "I just can't believe how beautiful it is," I finally say, looking at him in wonder.

He just nods.

"But . . . aren't you kind of sad to know that in just five more days it'll all be knocked down? Reduced to a pile of dust and memory?" I gaze back and forth, between the walls and him, trying to imagine the moment when all of this beauty he worked so hard to create will no longer exist.

But he just looks at me, squinting one eye and staring into mine. "Memories are the only things we really own, the only things that stay constant." He shrugs. "Everything else becomes dust."

And I just stand there, looking at him. And then I gaze once more at these incredible walls. And then I turn and head for the door.

Because I finally know what I have to do.

And just as I step outside, I turn back and poke my head in. "Um, I was just wondering, well, I don't even know your real name," I say, embarrassed to finally be admitting this.

But he just looks at me and nods. "George," he says, turning back toward the wall, lifting his brush to continue his story.

FROM: ELEANOR RIGBY
TO: CALVIN BURKE
SUBJECT: YOUR OFFER

Dear Mr. Burke,
I regret to inform you that for personal reasons I cannot divulge at this time, I am no longer able to accept your offer. Though I do thank you for thinking of me, and wish you all the best in your future projects.

Sincerely,
Eleanor Rigby

Twenty-seven

The second I sign off Autumn comes into our room, sees me on the computer, and goes, "So, any more secrets?"

And I totally freeze. And then I look at her, and go, "Huh?" And then I try to scrunch up my face like a person who was truly confused might. Even though I know I totally suck at things like this.

But she just sits on her bed, takes off her shoes, and goes, "Enough already, I know it's you." Then she levels her gaze, looking me right in the eye.

And even though I know I can probably drag this out awhile longer by going, "You know what's me?" and just repeating all of the same words right back at her until one of us gets bored and gives up. The fact is, this is Autumn I'm talking to here, the twelve-year-old sage who's light-years ahead of me. So instead I just shrug and say, "How'd you know?"

And she shakes her head, and rolls her eyes, and goes, "Oh, please. It's so obvious."

But I need a little more than that. Because even as smart as she is, if Autumn knows, then there's still a small chance that there may be others. "No, really," I say. "What exactly gave it away? What was it that tipped you off?"

And this time when she looks at me, she also laughs. "Okay first of all, Eleanor Rigby? Please. I mean, *come on*, Winter. Who else would know that song? Mom only played it like all day every day for the month and a half after she and Dad first split. And skinny smoker dude? We've already covered that. So obvious. Not to mention how you practically couldn't wait to tell me all about the breast enhancer–chicken cutlet fiasco like seconds after it happened." She shakes her head. "But even after all that, I still checked the history trail just to make sure. Guess Mom was a little late on buying us separate laptops, huh?"

"Oh, jeez, who else knows?" I ask, feeling a little panicky now, not to mention kind of dumb for thinking I'd been so subversive and elusive, when the whole time a sixth grader was on to me from the very start. "You didn't mention your theory to anyone else did you?" I look at her.

"Relax." She shrugs. "As far as I know, you're safe."

And then suddenly, I realize, that for the first time in a long time, I really do feel safe. It's like, now that my secret's out, now that I confessed and got it all off my chest, I feel lighter, less burdened, more like the old me, only better.

I mean, who would've thought that keeping your own secrets could turn out to be such a heavy load?

Then I log into my e-mail and show her the one from Calvin Burke.

And after she reads it, she just stares at me, with her eyes all wide and full of questions.

So I show her my most recent response.

And this time when she looks at me, I can tell she approves. "You did the right thing," she says, before heading out the door.

I just sit there, rereading the e-mail, knowing she's right. I mean, if I had accepted Calvin Burke's offer and sold my story, there's no doubt that I'd be far richer, and far more popular than I ever could have imagined before.

But I also know that I would have gotten there the exact same way that Sloane got to the top of Table A—by selling out my values and beliefs, and by slamming an old and trusted friend.

And tell me, where's the good karma in that?

Twenty-eight

I can't believe I forgot to mention this before, but Easton is also coming to the party. And even though I know how it seems like that might be a big deal, and like something that I couldn't possibly forget, the truth is, that it's really not such a big deal, and I truly did forget. I mean, Easton and I are definitely still really good friends, but that's about all. Because I think we're both pretty clear on the fact that even though we had some fun, shared some laughs, and made out a little, the big, serious romantic attraction just isn't there.

It's like, he's just looking to meet new people and have a good time. And I'm so lame and useless that I can't even muster the courage to talk to the guy who risked a personal social exile by getting on stage in front of the entire student body and dedicating a song that practically nobody knows, to a girl that practically nobody cares about. And even though I'm fully aware of how the door really doesn't open any wider than that,

I'm so freaking pathetic that I can't even ring the bell, much less go inside.

So a couple days ago when Easton called to tell me he had a small part in some indie film and would be shooting in and around Orange County for a few weeks, I just happened to mention my mom's New Year's bash and invited him to stop by. Then I gave him the details, closed the phone, and forgot all about it, until now.

But even though I'm not really all that into him, that doesn't mean I don't want him to be into me. Or, at least think I look good, or hot, or at the very minimum not be embarrassed to remember how he once made out with me.

So with Autumn's help, I pull together an outfit he's never seen before, black leggings, vintage silver sequin mini-dress, and spiky black ankle boots. And then when I'm done getting dressed, I gawk in amazement when she puts on a new dress.

"Oh, my, is that for little Crosby Davis?" I ask, thinking how pretty she can be when she's not all hippie-bohoed out.

"No. First it's for me. Then it's for Mom. Then it's for Boyd." She smiles shyly.

"Uh, who's Boyd?" I ask, watching her closely.

"The new kid," she says, slipping her feet into her new, mini-wedge heeled sandals.

The second I walk in the door, I scan the room for Rey. I mean, I'm kind of hoping I can talk to him before he gets too busy with the band, not to mention before I chicken out and lose my nerve completely. But, of course, now that I've finally found the words, he's not around to hear them.

So I try to look busy by rearranging the plates and cups (even though my eyes keep darting toward the door), and when Dave walks in he kisses my mom, and her face lights up brighter than the Fashion Island Christmas tree. Then he picks her up and spins her around, making her beautiful new dress rise up in a circle. And when I catch a glimpse of her un-shaven legs, I breathe a sigh of relief. Because even though I've pretty much made peace with all of her recent renovations, there's still this small part of me that needs her to be my same old mom.

And as the room starts to fill with just about every single person we know (and definitely a few that we don't), I'm feel-ing so anxious to find Rey and finally say my piece, that I don't even notice Easton until his arms are wrapped around my waist, and he's kissing the side of my neck.

"Hey," he whispers, leaning back and smiling.

And just as I start to push him away, I glance toward the door and see Rey.

And he's talking to Sloane.

And she reaches out to touch his arm at the exact same mo-ment that she dips her head, gazes up at him, and then tosses her hair so that it misses her shoulder and falls back over her eyes. Which happens to be a move that is well known to me, as I helped her perfect it last summer in our cocreated Flirting 101 seminar.

So, instinctively, without even thinking, I grab Easton and hug him again, making sure to lean in just a little bit more than I should, lingering like that until I'm sure Rey has seen us.

"So, help yourself to some food and drink," I say, suddenly sounding all perfunctory and businesslike. I mean, now that Rey is safely away from Sloane, and up onstage doing a sound check I'm pretty much over the need for any further displays of affection.

"I'm good for now," Easton says, slipping his arm around my waist just as Sloane and her posse approach.

"Omigod, this is *so* great!" Sloane says, her mouth bestow-ing me with her most winning smile, while her eyes offer a pretty harsh look for someone who supposedly loves my party.

I smile at her, then gaze at her posse, all three of who are totally checking out Easton. So I go, "Easton, this is Sloane, Jaci, Holly, and Claire."

He nods distractedly, and pulls me even closer.

But this is not a group of girls who are used to being ignored. And believe me, to them, rejection is so not an option. So Jaci steps forward, and pressing her fingertips lightly to his sleeve says, "Oh, I love your shirt! So soft!" And she stands there, stroking the fabric between her thumb and index finger, and smiling at him like an open invitation.

So of course, not to be outdone by anyone, especially her competitive clone, Sloane grabs his hand and goes, "I've never seen you before. What school do you go to?"

And when he tells her, she turns and looks at me, narrowing her eyes and pursing her lips with visibly seething anger. As though I somehow owe her an explanation of how I could possibly know two hot guys when I didn't use to know anyone but her.

"So how'd you guys meet?" she asks, glancing from me to him, her eyes working overtime, attempting to calculate something that, in her mind, just doesn't compute.

So I look at Easton and he looks at me and then I don't even know why but we both start cracking up, while Sloane and her friends just stand there, looking at us like we're crazy or something. Well, actually, they're looking at *me* like *I'm* crazy. Because as far as they're concerned, Easton is still the hot and mysterious stranger.

But when I finally stop laughing, Sloane is still glaring at me. And it makes me wonder why she just had to come to my party if all she plans to do is shoot eyeball daggers my way. So feeling pretty anxious to get far away from her, I just go, "We met in New York. But Easton can tell it way better than me." Then I excuse myself and head for the other side of the room, hoping to put some distance between us.

The first song Social Exile performs is "Cinnamon Girl." And even though I know it's for my mom, because let's face it, she's the one that's paying them, and only her and her friends (and freaks who have no choice like Autumn and I) even know that song to begin with, I'd be totally lying if I tried to pretend I wasn't hoping it would be my song. Or our song. Or "A Hazy Shade of Winter." Or whatever. And when I look around I see Autumn and her two best friends dancing together, just laughing and having fun. But I also notice how every few seconds Autumn glances over at this cute little sixth grader, who's trying so hard to look cool, even though he's peeking at her, too.

And all I can think is, *Oh, jeez, it's already starting.*

Then I see my mom and Dave, holding hands and talking to some friends, and she looks more happy and radiant than I've ever seen her before. And then I see Hayden gazing at Mick as he plays the guitar, and Elijah pretending like he's listening to Evan and Clark even though he's actually watching Hayden gaze at Mick. And when Easton comes over, slides his arm around my waist, and asks me if I want to dance, I just shake my head and walk away.

And just as I'm about to head into the back room so I can chill by myself for a while, I'm cornered by Sloane, Jaci, Holly, and Claire. And by the way they're surrounding me, it's clear it's no accident.

"Oh, hey," I say, stopping just shy of the door, wondering what they could possibly want. I mean, Sloane's hands are on her hips and her eyes are all narrowed into angry little slits, as her posse remains on standby, poised and ready to act on a moment's notice.

"You must think you're really fucking brilliant, huh?" Sloane says, her face a visible scowl, her right, stiletto-clad foot tapping ominously against the concrete floor.

But I just look at her and shrug. Because even though I

really don't think I'm all that brilliant, I am smart enough to know that answering a question like that is just totally asking for it.

"You must think you're just so fucking funny, and clever, and witty, and mysterious. *Don't you?*" she says, still glaring at me.

Okay, this is getting creepy. I mean, I have no idea what she's talking about. But from the expressions on Jaci, Holly, and Claire's faces, it's pretty clear that I'm not the only one who's confused by all this. So finally I just shrug and say, "Um, I really don't know what your deal is, but I think I'll be going now." Then I turn and reach for the doorknob.

"Um, hello? Your stupid fucking *blog,* Winter, that's what I'm talking about. Or should I call you *Eleanor Rigby?*"

Oh, great. I clutch the handle, feeling my palm grow wet and slippery against the metal as my stomach drops to my knees.

"Did you think I wouldn't find out? Did you think I'm too fucking dumb to recognize myself? *Did you think I was too fucking stupid to realize that I'm Princess Pink?*"

"I . . ." I turn and look at her, unable to finish that thought. Because the truth is, I really did think all that. Though apparently I was wrong.

And then just as I'm about to offer an apology for betraying her like that, and maybe even try to explain my side of things, Jaci, Holly, and Claire take one look at her and go, *"You're* Princess Pink?" Followed by:

"Omigod, *you* made out with your cousin?"

"*You* used lip gloss that fell in the toilet?"

"*You* made flash cards? That is so fucking retarded!" Jaci says, moving away from her and shaking her head in disgust.

"Ew!" Holly and Claire cringe, backing away from her as though all of those sad little secrets are somehow contagious.

As I just stand there, watching Sloane get dumped by the friends she worked so hard to get. And I gotta admit, even though Sloane's a total bitch, and even though she betrayed me first, it still feels pretty awful to realize that everything that's happening here is happening because of me.

"She's a fucking liar!" Sloane points at me, her face turning a bright, panicked red, as she suddenly realizes she just outed herself. "None of that is true! *None of it!*"

But it's too late for that, because Jaci, Holly, and Claire aren't buying it. They just stand there shaking their heads and smirking at Sloane, pity and disgust shaping their faces as Sloane stands before them, shaking with rage.

"Oh, screw you! You think I don't know you put that note on my butt?" She points at Jaci. "You think I don't know that all of you are responsible for writing trash about me on those bathroom walls?" She shakes her head and glares at them, smirking as they cringe in shame. But I can tell it's more the shame of getting caught, as opposed to any real, moral kind. "You're all jealous! That's your problem. Every single one of you wishes you were me and you know it!" she says, her voice a scary, harsh whisper.

"Uh, whatever." Jaci rolls her eyes and veers for the front door while Holly and Claire trail closely behind. "Good luck Monday at school," they say.

Sloane turns toward me, her face red with anger, her eyes squinting back tears. "Happy? I mean, this is what you wanted, right?"

"Sloane—" I start to say, but then stop. Because the truth is, this is *exactly* what I wanted. Only now that it's all mission accomplished, I'm really not feeling all that great about it.

"You think you won this one, right? Well, think again. I didn't work this hard, and come this far to be brought down by a loser like you! I'm gonna make you so fucking sorry." She glares at me.

I just stand there looking at her. "I already am," I whisper, watching as she storms away from me, and heads straight for Easton.

When I finally get into the back room, I plop down onto the old worn-out couch and drop my head in my hands. And no matter how hard I try to block it out, all I can hear is the sound of my mom's voice echoing, "Be careful what you wish for, you just might get it." Which is what she repeated to Autumn and me more times than I care to count. And yet, maybe she was right. Because so far practically everything I've wished for *has* come true. And to be honest, most of it's not near as great as I hoped it would be. In fact, most of it's not even close.

I rest my head against the cushions, and run my fingers over the old, worn corduroy fabric, thinking about how much everything has changed, and how this fossilized couch is now one of the last remaining relics of our old life. And I can't help but wonder if my mom's planning to throw it out, too. And suddenly the thought of losing this butt-ugly, yet completely precious sofa makes me feel so unbelievably empty and sad that I suddenly break down in a flood of uncontrollable, unstoppable tears.

Yup, that's right, I start sobbing over a couch.

When I finally quiet down to just a few residual sniffles, I reach for the old, three-shades-of-blue afghan blanket that my grandma knit for me not long before she died, wrap it around me, grab my cell phone, and call my dad.

And when his phone goes straight into voice mail, I can't say I'm surprised. I mean, he's a celebrity now, so I'm sure he's busy being famous somewhere. So I leave a message, wishing him a wonderful New Year, and telling him how much I love and appreciate him, and how because of all that I've decided to make myself available for *Act II,* season two, and anything else he might need. I mean, I'm going to have a stepdad soon, and even though Dave's like a really cool guy, he's not my real dad. And it's not like he could ever replace him.

I mean, at one point when we were in the back room, kiss-
on the old corduroy couch, he pulled away and looked at
. And this time he insisted on talking.

"Winter," he said, shaking his head and peering at me. "I
ve liked you this whole entire time. Ever since that day you
n into me in the hall."

But just because I knew he was telling the truth, doesn't
mean I knew how to respond. So I just sat there, listening to his
words, but not contributing any of my own.

"And I tried to make it clear, I mean I tried so many times
to let you know how I felt, but you were so preoccupied with
Sloane and Cash and all that other stuff, that I finally just gave
up. Because I knew there was just no way I could compete with
all that."

And even though I knew this to be true, I refused to let
him off that easy. "But you're the one who invited Shay to the
Dirty Bird that night, not me," I finally said, speaking up in
my own defense.

But he just looked at me, and shook his head. "That was a
pathetic, last-minute attempt to get your attention. And when
it failed, I decided it was time to move on."

And not knowing what else to say, I tried to just lean in
and kiss him again. But he stopped me. Holding my face in his
hands, he looked me in the eye, and said, "Winter, I'm serious."

And then, pressing my lips against his, I whispered, "Rey,
me too."

TO: ELEANOR RIGBY
FROM: CALVIN BURKE
RE: PLEASE RECONSIDER

Dear Ms. Rigby:
Please forgive my tardy response as I was out of the
country for several weeks and have only just returned to find
your e-mail. I am sorry to read that you are unable to accept

Then I snap my phone shut, toss it back in my purse, tuck
the blanket under my feet, and drift.

I guess I must have dozed off for a while, because when I
open my eyes again, I can hear someone else in the room. And
after squinting and adjusting to the dim light, I realize it's
Rey.

"Sorry, I didn't mean to wake you," he says, pilfering quietly through his backpack.

But I just sit up and glance around, wondering how long
I'd been sleeping. Then I look at him and say, "You guys
sounded really good out there." I push my hair off of my face
and smile.

But he just laughs and goes, "Yeah, I can see that, with the
way you were sleeping and all."

But I don't want him to think that his music sucks, so I go,
"No, really, I was just—" But then I stop, deciding to let the
sentence end there. Because even though I don't want him to
think that his music put me to sleep, I also realize that I can't
exactly confide in him about how I just battled my way
through a severe emotional meltdown over an old, sagging,
brown corduroy couch.

And just as he grabs the door handle, ready to head back
out, he turns and looks at me. "Should I tell Easton you're
here?"

And when I look at him, I realize it's actually a much bigger question than it might seem. I also know that it's now or
never. That if I mess this one up, he'll walk out that door, and I
may never get a chance to really talk to him again. And even
though there are so many things I want to tell him, now that
it's time, I can't seem to find the right words. But even if I
could, I doubt that the lump in my throat would allow me to
say them.

So I just shake my head in a silent good-bye.

But then, the next thing I know, he's sitting right beside

me, and he's kissing me. And even though this may be hard to believe, I'm totally not exaggerating when I say that it's even better than the first time.

Then he pulls away, looks in my eyes, and says, "Winter, I—"

But I press my finger to his lips, stopping his words as I lean in to kiss him again. Because right now I don't want to hear anything. I just want *this*.

Twenty-nine

By the very last set, I'm up onstage, having reinstated my ro. as backup singer for the band. And I just stand there, nodding my head to the beat, waiting my turn to sing, as I watch Autumn dance awkwardly (but happily!) with Boyd, as Sloane engages in a full-scale seduction of Easton, attaching herself to his body, while glaring at me from over his shoulder.

I guess once she learned that he was a *working actor,* currently cast in an indie film, it was good-bye, Rey, hello, Sundance Film Festival.

And even though part of me is bugged when I watch just how much pleasure she takes in stealing the guy she thinks I'm with, the other part feels pretty good when I realize just how easy it was to dupe her. And how Easton is really just a decoy for the ultimate catch I was after.

And not that I want to move too quickly, or make any kind of crazy, false assumptions, but I think it might actually be safe to say that Rey is now officially my boyfriend.

my offer and am hoping that I can persuade you to please reconsider. I have already spoken with a few publishers, all of whom have shown interest in your story, and once the book rights are sold, I plan to move on to film.

I'm sure you're aware of the level of competition, and that opportunities like this don't come around often.

I hope I've managed to regain your interest, and that you will soon contact me at your earliest convenience. I look forward to working with you.

Sincerely,
Calvin Burke

Wednesday, January 10, 2007

4:45 P.M.

Current Mood—In love!

Current Music—"A Hazy Shade of Winter" by my ultimate, all-time, favorite indie band

Quote of the Day—"Be who you are and say what you feel, because those who mind don't matter, and those who matter don't mind."—Dr. Seuss

It's My Life

Spotted: the girl formerly known as Princess Pink, but now better known as Social Casualty #1, sitting alone, and deflecting glares, jeers, and heckles from her former friends and Pastel Posse members, while her thumbs twitch like crazy as she furiously text messages mysterious someone. Could it be Mr. Hollywood from the New Year's Eve midnight make-out?

We may never know.

Because it's a new year, and I'm moving on to new things. Which means I will no longer be spying on, obsessing over, or spilling any more of P. P.'s secrets. Or anyone else's secrets. Which also means there will be no book deal, no Podcast, and no big-screen adaptation (sorry C. B.), and no more blog entries.

I mean, I think I might have actually learned a few things last year. Like: people change, secrets are sacred, and that with the right people in attendance, even the lowliest lunch table can feel like the warmest place on the planet.

And so I say good-bye. Though I thank you for all of your comments and support, and for joining me on this amazing journey. And now that I'm ready to go it alone, I wish you all the best on yours.

Your friend,

Eleanor Rigby

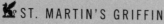

From the #1 New York Times *bestselling author
of* **the immortals** *comes a breathtaking
new series brimming with magic, mystery,
and an intoxicating love story that will
steal your heart away.*
Meet **the soul seekers**.

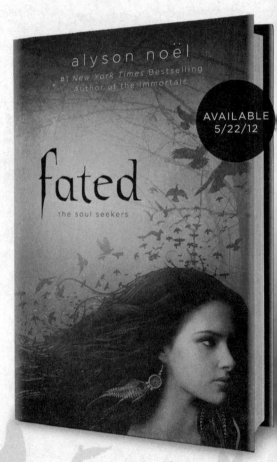

AVAILABLE
5/22/12

Haunted by strange
dreams, Daire goes to
live with her grandmother,
who recognizes what's
truly happening. Daire
is being called to her
destiny as a Soul Seeker—
one who can navigate
between the worlds of
the living and dead.

On the dusty plains of
Enchantment, New Mexico,
Daire meets Dace, the
boy from her dreams.
And she'll have to discover
if he's the one . . . or
if he's the enemy she's
destined to destroy.

Read on for a glimpse of *fated*,
book one of **the soul seekers**!

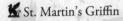 St. Martin's Griffin

A GLIMPSE OF

fated

AVAILABLE
MAY 2012

The boy calls after me as I shove through crowds of people my age. Knocking into girls and bouncing off boys, until one in particular catches me, steadies me. His fingers circling my arm as he peers down and says, "You okay?"

I struggle against him, fight to break free. Though it's not long before I'm overcome by a cool wash of calm chased by a comforting warmth that folds like a blanket around me. My movements slowed, my thoughts becoming so hazy and loose, I abandon my flight. Robbed of all recollection of why I wanted to leave when I'd do anything to always feel so secure—so safe—so loved and at peace.

So at home in his arms.

I melt against his chest—lift my gaze to meet his. Gasping when I stare into a pair of icy-blue eyes banded by brilliant flecks of gold that shine like kaleidoscopes, reflecting my image thousands of times.

The boy from my dream.

The one who died in my arms.

the soul seekers series
Fated, available May 2012
Echo, available Fall 2012
Mystic, available Spring 2013
Horizon, available Fall 2013

Enter the world of
the immortals

BOOK 4 — dark flame

BOOK 5 — night star · a novel · the immortals

BOOK 6 — everlasting · a novel

BOOK 1 — evermore · a novel · the immortals

BOOK 2 — blue moon · a novel · the immortals

BOOK 3 — shadowland · a novel · the immortals

alyson noël

"Addictive. I couldn't put it down. I dreamt about this book. And when I was finished, I couldn't get it out of my head. Simply breathtaking." —*Teens Read Too* on *Evermore*

For free downloads, hidden surprises, and glimpses into the future

Visit www.ImmortalsSeries.com.